SHOTGUN MARSHAL

Wade Everett

GUNSMOKE

First published in the UK by Collins

This hardback edition 2009
by BBC Audiobooks Ltd
by arrangement with
Golden West Literary Agency

ISBN 978 1 405 68258 9

British Library Cataloguing in Publication Data available.

Printed and bound in Great Britain by
CPI Antony Rowe, Chippenham and Eastbourne

SHOTGUN MARSHAL

Chapter One

At a quarter to seven, Adam Collier kissed his wife, hoisted his seven-year-old daughter to his shoulders, and walked to his front gate with each of the five-year-old twin boys, standing on his insteps and clinging to his legs. At the gate, which was as far as the children were allowed to go after sunset, he stopped, kissed the girl, gave the boys playful thumps on their bottoms and sent them back to the house.

Then he walked on down the street, hands in his pockets, pipe clenched between his teeth. He was thirty-one, a firm-bodied man in a blue uniform with a round, billed fireman's cap squared on his head.

Collier lived at the edge of town and, each evening, if the windows were closed and the pump organ was played loud enough, a good deal of the noise of Gold Street was shut out. But, as he walked along, heading for Gold Street, the din mounted steadily, a blend of men shouting, noisy pianos from the solid line of saloons, and the shrill laughter of women from the cribs behind the street.

He reached the west end of Gold Street, an eight-block avenue of dust braced on both sides by places that rarely closed. Men and horses filled the street, crowded the walks, and as Adam Collier walked along, he had to side-step often to avoid collisions with men bent on their headlong ways.

Halfway down, he cut over a block and walked up a steep street sided by the county building, the fire station and marshal's office. The men on duty at the station were lined up in front of it, chairs tipped back against the brick wall. He stopped a moment to pass the time, then walked on and went into the courthouse, a three-story stone building with the jail occupying most of the basement floor.

He went up the broad stairs and through a wide oak door as the town clock struck seven, a gentle pealing that was swallowed up by the noise of Gold Street. There were five men seated around a long table in the room he entered. Adam Collier took his place.

Jim Enright, mayor of Bonanza, said, "Stiles and Bridges will be a little late, Adam. They're having supper at the hotel with the new marshal."

Pete Madden, sitting across from Collier, said, "I get to treat the next one. Two in one year is some kind of a record."

"Especially when two are dead and buried," Enright commented.

Enright was a man of fifty with a wide expanse of stomach encased in an embroidered vest and spanned by a gold link watch chain. "You've got a wide-open town and you have to expect a certain degree of trouble. This man is good. Experienced. And he brings a reputation with him."

"Who needs it?" Pete Madden asked. "The town's got a big one now."

Madden, a man in his late thirties, rather thin in the face, ran the assay office, which was a very profitable business in a gold town where every man either dug ore or looked for it or stole it.

The door opened and Jeff Stiles and Howard Bridges came in; they sat down immediately and unbuttoned their coats and vests.

Adam Collier asked, "Where is this stalwart tower of law and order, Jeff?"

"Outside." Jeff smiled, showing many gold teeth. "Gentlemen, we have made no mistake this time. We've got a real ripsnorting buckaroo."

"I think it's time we invited Mr. Beal in to talk this over," Mayor Enright said. "Jeff?"

Stiles got up, opened the door and crooked his finger. The men all turned so they could see Joe Beal. He stopped in the doorway as though he were suspicious of the room and the people in it. He was a shade over six feet, wide in the shoulders; he wore a dark suit with the tails swept back from a pair of pearl-handled pistols which roosted on his hips. His shirt had laces at the throat and cuffs. He put his beaver on the table before looking around.

Jeff Stiles made the introductions. "Gentlemen, I'd like to present Joe Beal, late of Abilene, Hays City. At the end of the table, Jim Enright, mayor of Bonanza. On his right, Pete Madden, our assayer. Across the table, Adam Collier, of our fire department."

Beal nodded briefly for each of the introductions and Stiles went on while Collier studied Beal. The new marshal had a broad, expressionless face, the kind a man needed for a high-stake poker game. His eyes were dark, quick-moving, and, when Collier looked into them, they told him nothing. The introductions over, Beal sat down.

Enright said, "I see no reason we can't discuss details. You agree to the salary?"

"If I understand it right," Beal said. "One hundred and fifty dollars a month and fifty per cent of the fines."

"That's correct," Enright said. He opened his mouth to go on, but Beal cut him off.

"Who gets the other fifty per cent?"

"Why, I do," Enright said, surprised. "For the administration of my office." He waited for some comment; when there was none, he continued, "The city will pay for two full-time deputies at a hundred dollars a month each."

"If I need any, I'll hire them," Beal stated. "Who feeds the prisoners?"

"You do."

Beal shook his head. "That's no good. I usually have a full jail."

Enright looked around, and Howard Bridges said, "I make a motion the city feed the prisoners."

The motion was seconded and passed, with Adam Collier voting against it. This drew Beal's attention.

"Don't you believe in cooperating with a man, Mr. Fireman?" Beal asked.

"I like to make sure I know what I'm doing when I vote."

"What are you, a little slow or something?" Beal asked. "I just told you why I wanted it."

"Sometimes a man just doesn't get everything he wants."

"Let's not have a debate," Enright suggested. "I'm sure Mr. Beal has many questions he'd like answered about our town."

"A few," Beal said. "First, I want to know who to leave alone."

"Roan Spencer owns the Occidental mine. I would treat him and his foreman with a good deal of respect," Enright mentioned. "You might accord Fred Carlyle the same treatment. He owns the Golden Kate, another large mine."

"Who runs the gambling in town? The cribs? I want to know the people I'm not supposed to have trouble with."

Enright seemed embarrassed. "Why, what makes you think——"

"Somebody pays the piper in this town and the cash lines someone's pockets," Beal stated bluntly. "I don't want to bite the hand that feeds me."

There was silence, broken by Adam Collier when he scratched a match on the underside of the table to light his pipe. He smiled through a cloud of smoke and laughed. "He walks in here cold and sees it, Jim, but you go on telling me it doesn't show. I'm telling you again to get this town cleaned up."

"I'll do that," Beal said.

"Not if you're going to take graft to turn your back on the alley blackjackings and robbery," Collier said.

Beal turned in his chair to look squarely at Adam Collier; he had a habit of turning his upper body instead of just his head. "If you're so against all this, why the hell haven't you done something?"

"No backing," he said. "Enright keeps insisting that these things are part of growing pains, part of a seven-thousand-population town that's splitting us out at the seams. Then, too, there are some risks." He looked briefly around the table. "We've had some honest men wearing the badge here. They're dead."

"They're dead and I get a job," Beal said. "I can't cry over that. You still haven't answered my question."

"We don't know," Enright said simply. "It's a fact, but we just don't know."

"You can't think I'm stupid enough to believe that, do you?" Beal replied. "I'll tell you now, you level with me or you can have the job. I've got to know who to leave alone, who not to turn my back on. It's no matter to me who you make your deals with. But I make my deals with *you*, and they'd better be straight." He put his hands flat on the table and waited. "Don't take up too much of my time, gentlemen."

"Be careful now," Adam Collier warned. "We just look soft." He took his pipe out of his mouth and leaned forward. "There isn't a man sitting at this table who's taken a dollar or a dime from the criminals in this town. There isn't a man here who hasn't asked himself and the others a hundred times who runs these things. We've suspected law officers of falling in with these people, but we've buried two, so it makes us wonder." He shrugged and spread his hands. "That's it, Beal. Take it or leave it."

"Well, someone bosses this town," Beal said. "And I'll find out who."

"And do what?" Collier asked.

Beal's glance came around. "I didn't like that."

"So? That the first thing in your life you didn't like?"

"I don't think I'm going to like you," Beal said. "And if my jail catches fire, I may not even call you because of it." He suddenly tipped his chair back and laughed. "I don't scare you a damned bit, do I, Collier?"

"Not a bit."

"I like that," Beal admitted. "We'll get along." He stood up. "When can I be sworn in?"

"Judge Waller will do it tonight," Enright said. "Jeff, get the newspaper editor out of the Jackpot and have him bring his camera and we'll meet at Waller's house in a half hour." He rapped his gavel. "I'll entertain a motion for adjournment."

The meeting broke up with a scraping of chairs. Stiles left to make the arrangements.

Howard Bridges spoke to Adam Collier. "Coming over to the judge's house?"

"No, I'll go on home."

Collier put his pipe in his pocket and settled his cap squarely on his head. Beal was standing nearby; the pearl handles of his guns catching the lamplight prompted Collier to speak. "If I had your job I wouldn't wear two pistols. It's a theory of mine, untested, of course, but, when a man wears a gun, it's only a matter of time before he has to use it."

"I know how to use mine," Beal said. "And I'd bet I can use it better than the next man." He took a cigar from his pocket and offered it to Collier, who shook his head. "Would you like a drink before going home?"

"Thanks, I would," Collier said and went to the door.

Enright called, "Don't be late at the judge's house, Mr. Beal."

"I'm never late for anything," Beal told him and went out with Collier. They walked a block over to the main street and eased their way through the dense traffic on the walk. Collier led as they went down to the Jackpot. The doors of the saloon were constantly in motion and they had to wait a short time before they could make their way inside.

Collier shunned the bar which was lined five deep its entire length. Six bartenders perspired as they worked. He led the way to Bill Frame's office in the back, knocked, then stepped inside when he heard Frame speak.

Frame was at his desk, pouring a drink. He was in his shirt sleeves; his tie was askew, one cuff was torn, and there was a trickle of blood at the corner of his mouth. A man in a frock coat was pulling himself up from the floor and trying to stop the blood flowing from his nose at the same time.

"Now, get out!" Frame shouted. "Take your cards someplace else and play where the house rules are more relaxed."

The man stumbled to the door, brushing Collier as he went out.

Frame smiled and said, "You missed the party."

Frame tossed off his drink and took off his torn shirt. He was a bit over thirty, a solid man with heavy muscles and a firm, square face. He got another shirt out of the closet and put it on.

"He was dealing for the house and cheating," Frame explained. "He'll have another job inside an hour." He looked at Joe Beal. "Are you the man Enright sent for?"

Collier introduced them. "Joe Beal—Bill Frame, who *does* run an honest saloon—I think the only one in Bonanza."

"And how's business?" Beal asked.

"I get the big share," Frame admitted. "I believe

an honest man will always make more money than a crook in the long run. A drink?"

"That's what we came for," Collier admitted and sat down.

Frame set out the glasses and poured, then leaned on the corner of his desk. "Mr. Beal, here's luck on the job. It's a wild town. Sometimes I think the council runs it, then, again, I don't know who does. For sure, no one's been able to quiet it down. The decent people lock their doors at sundown. A man takes his chances just walking the street, especially if he's carrying a poke. I keep two shotgun guards on duty every night just to walk home my heavy winners. So far, no one has been robbed when he had a shotgun escort. That's the kind of a town it is, Marshal."

"I knew it was anything but a tame pigeon when I left Kansas," Beal said. He looked at Collier, then at Bill Frame. "You two long-time friends?"

"Twelve years," Frame said. "Since '61. We were in the army together, served in the same regiment. Got our promotions together; got out together; and came here together."

Beal nodded. "To stay alive in my work, a man has to know who he can trust and who he can't. If I get into a corner in your place, what can I expect, Mr. Frame?"

"Out there on the floor, perched on high stools, are three shotgun guards. They see just about everything. I keep four bouncers on duty around the clock. If there's anything they can't handle, the shotgun guards move in. There have been no killings in my place for nearly two years. If you got in a tight one here, the establishment will back you. Beal, the real bad ones stay clear of my place. They've learned that."

Beal said, "Now if I can only convince the bad ones that Bonanza is a poor town to live in, we'll be getting somewhere."

"That's about the job you took," Collier said.

Beal looked at him. "What kind of a fire-fighting force do you have in this town?"

"Twenty-four men in three shifts," Collier said. "Why—you thinking of burning the place down?"

"No," Beal said softly. "I was thinking of something else. Like—if we needed them, could we make them into a temporary police force?" He shrugged. "Just a thought. Maybe I'll talk to the mayor about it."

"Talk to me," Collier advised. "I run the fire department."

"Well, I just might at that," Joe Beal admitted. "Good whiskey."

Chapter Two

Judge Waller lived in a small frame house on the west edge of town. Adam Collier went with Joe Beal to show him the way and to be present when Bonanza's new marshal was being sworn in. Jim Enright and several others were in the judge's parlor when they arrived.

Clyde Meers, who ran the newspaper, was there with his camera and boxes of chemicals and eternal odor of whiskey; he drank continuously and his eyes were always a little bloodshot, yet whiskey never affected him to the point where he made printing errors or failed to publish the truth. Beal was taken into tow by Enright immediately upon arrival.

Adam Collier walked over to where Meers was setting up his equipment. "If you had to take a picture in a hurry you'd be in trouble, wouldn't you?"

Meers smiled. "You want to know something, Adam? I'm in trouble even without this thing. When I bought it, I was going to be another Brady and capture the face of the world on a glass plate. Stupid idea, like most that I get." He ducked under the hood to focus and adjust, then reappeared. "What kind of a man are we hiring this time?"

"Tough, and I think honest."

"Tough, we've had before," Meers said. "Honest, I've never been sure."

"You wouldn't trust your mother."

"You must know my mother to say that," Meers commented. He clapped his hands. "Gentlemen, if you'll stand over there by those atrocious drapes, I'll make sure I have you all in the picture. Adam?"

"Thanks, no, I'll stand this one out. People will see my picture in the paper and think I'm running for public office." He smiled and went over and leaned against a far wall and smoked his pipe.

Judge Waller placed the men, then patted the roundness of his stomach and brushed his beard with his fingers. He tried to stretch his five-feet-eight into something a little more impressive while Meers made his final adjustments. The newsman held aloft his tray of flash powder and when it whoofed and belched smoke they all jumped, but their images had been captured.

Meers got out his pad and pencil and said, "All right, Judge, let's have the speech."

"Why, I had no—ah, yes, perhaps a few words."

The judge swore Joe Beal in and pinned the badge on him while Meers walked over and stood by Adam Collier. Judge Waller rambled on about the town and the promise it held for everyone; Meers put away his notebook. Collier saw this and bent to whisper in the newspaperman's ear.

"Aren't you going to write it down?"

"That garbage? Who'd read it?

Meers spoke his mind aloud and Waller stopped talking and turned his head and glared, then went on.

"Windbag," Meers said.

Waller concluded his remarks, shook hands all

around, and then poured drinks. When he gave Meers his glass, he said, "You're an extremely rude man, Clyde. On several occasions I've had a mind to cane you."

"I've been buggy-whipped twice this last year and beaten once," Meers admitted. "I think I could survive a caning. Is this your good whiskey or the bottle you keep for guests?"

"If this weren't official, you wouldn't be welcome in my house, sir!"

"If it weren't official, I wouldn't want to come here," Meers told him.

Waller closed his eyes for an instant and muttered something. Then he turned back to his guests, leaving Collier and Meers alone.

Meers said, "You've always seemed to be able to stand me, Adam. What's the matter with you? A little stupid in the head?"

"I suppose that's the case," Collier admitted. "Clyde, when you have trouble, why don't you ask for help?"

"I make my own trouble and I settle it myself." He smiled. "Not very well though. Don't have the size or weights for it. But we give it a try." He pushed away from the wall. "I'll pack this up and we can go to my office. I pour better whiskey than the judge does."

Adam Collier laughed and shook his head. "I've had two drinks already tonight and my wife doesn't like it when I smell like a hot mince pie."

"You're going home?" Meers asked, pretending shock.

"To the wife and kiddies."

He shook his head. "A picture of domestic bliss.

Go, then—with my sympathies, and perhaps a good deal of my envy."

Collier went over to Judge Waller and thanked him for his hospitality. He shook hands with Joe Beal and wished him well with the job. Then he left the house and walked down the dark street. The sky was clear and a sliver of moon shed some light along the street. Collier turned the corner at his street, then stopped when two horsemen rode by, edging close to the path in an attempt to identify him. This was enough to arouse Collier's suspicions and, as soon as the horsemen rode past, he jumped a low picket fence and went to a tree squatting in the middle of a lawn. He jumped up, grabbed a low stub of dead branch; he felt it give, then break, under his weight. With this in hand he went over the fence again and walked on.

The horsemen turned in mid-block and came back, staying to the center of the street. Collier watched them, giving them his full attention. When they were abreast of him and about to pass on, they both veered sharply and came at him, the horses lunging forward so that he would be pinned between the animals. Collier jumped to one side and swung his club, catching one man across the chest. The blow sounded like a drum with a soggy head being struck and the man grunted and flew over the rump of his horse.

Surprised, the second man wheeled his horse and came around again. Collier hit him a glancing blow on the head. The rider cried out and fell forward across the neck of his horse which broke into a run and disappeared down the street.

The downed man was trying to get up, but the

wind had been knocked out of him and he could only moan and paw the dirt with his feet. Adam Collier threw the club away and walked on toward his home, knowing that he would only be going to a lot of trouble if he took the man to jail and had him arrested. In the morning, Judge Waller would fine him five dollars; the fine would be paid and the man would go free.

It just wasn't worth a man's trouble.

There was lamplight shining through the lace curtains of his parlor window as he took his key from his pants pocket when he approached the porch. His wife, June, heard him unlocking the door; she came to the hallway to put her arms around him and kiss him.

"Is your civic duty all done?" she asked.

"For the night, anyway. Any coffee?"

"Yes, and some pie. Sit down and I'll get it for you." She was a slender, shapely woman in her late twenties, with rather pale brown hair and full lips accustomed to smiling.

Collier went to his favorite leather chair, put on his slippers, and refilled his pipe. She came back the coffee and pie on a tray and put it down on a table near him. Then June sat across from him.

"What's the new marshal like, Adam?"

"I think I like him. He's no fool. The others were. They were certain they could make Bonanza into a hymn-singing community. He doesn't believe that for a minute. He knows what a booming town is like, that there's crime and bad booze and crooked cards and plenty of painted ladies. He also knows there are decent, solid citizens who deserve protection." He picked up the pie and forked a piece into his mouth, then made a squint-eyed face indicating supreme pleasure. "June, when it comes to pie-baking and the begetting of children———"

"All right," she said, smiling. "I really don't know where the twins came from. There never have been any in my family, or in yours."

"True, but I was thinking that we might try again."

"Eat your pie," she said. "We can talk about that after you blow out the lamps."

At a quarter to one, a long time after Beal and Collier had left the Jackpot for Judge Waller's, Bill Frame left his saloon by the back way, walked the length of a dark alley, then turned left and started up the hill toward the line of bawdy houses. They sat shoulder to shoulder, shades drawn, red bull's-eye lanterns over the doors, and he passed a half dozen before turning into another alley. He got out of the dense pedestrian traffic that way; he moved along in the darkness until he came to a gap between two buildings. There was barely enough room for him to pass through sideways so he moved slowly until he came to a flush door. A key he held turned the lock. He stepped inside, closing the door, testing it to make sure it was locked.

The room Frame entered was small, eight by ten. He lighted a lamp. There was a barred cage only three-feet square but high enough for a man to stand in; the door of the cage was open. A chair stood in the cage.

Four lamps with polished reflectors which were on standards were focused on a small table and chair on the other side of the cage. Bill Frame put a match to the lamps, got them going, got them throwing their bright beams on the chair. Then he blew out the first lamp he had lit, stepped into the cage, and closed the door, sliding a bolt so that it could not be opened from the outside. He sat in complete darkness. No one could see him with the lamps focused as they were.

For five minutes he waited, then another door opened, one leading into the room from inside the building.

A tall, bearded man stepped in. "We've got him outside."

"Trouble?"

"No."

"Bring him in," Frame ordered. "Have three men come in with you. We don't know what he'll do."

The man stepped out and a moment later he came back, with three more men and Joe Beal. His pistol holsters were empty and he blinked at the bright glare of the mirrored lamplight.

"Sit down," Frame said, keeping his voice deep with even cadence. "May I congratulate you on your appointment?"

"You can go to hell," Beal said flatly. "I like to see a man when I talk to him."

"I'm afraid it's impossible in this case," Frame said. "And if you happen to remember this house and seek it out again, you won't find anything in this room that will tell you anything. So why don't you be sensible and sit down? Do I have to ask my friends to help you sit?"

Joe Beal knew when to be a fool and when not; he sat down and folded his hands. "All right, what's all the mystery?"

"No mystery; I prefer to remain anonymous. Mr.

Beal, as you are the new city marshal, I think it is very important that we have a business discussion."

"You want to find out how much of me you can buy?"

"Frankly, that's about it."

"You couldn't buy the other two so you had them killed," Beal said.

"Not quite like that," Frame admitted. "We bought them, but they got too big for their pants. You can get killed for that too."

"I guess." Beal stretched his long legs under the table, trying to feel what was beyond. He let none of this show on his face. "So, what's on your mind?"

"Let me explain how things are, Mr. Beal. In Bonanza, there are three kinds of people: those who work in the mines and make wages, those who work in the cribs and gambling places to take those wages, and those who only take the big winnings off the big winners. Now you must ask yourself, Mr. Beal, who actually gets caught? The train robbers, the bank robbers, the holdup men—they all get caught because they try to steal it all in one lump. The men of my organization don't go in for that at all. We wouldn't try to rob one of the mine payrolls or hold up a stage. That would be stupid. Neither would we molest the money in the local bank, or the weekly receipts at the stores. You see, there is no profit in holding up one man; he probably doesn't have any more than a week's pay in his pocket. Or he may have nothing, having lost his pay at cards or dice. So you're taking a lot of risks for very little. It is much more profitable to keep track of the games and when the big winner leaves, take him when he least expects it."

"All right. But where do I come in?" Beal asked.

"You're the law. We're in a risky business. Now and then, a victim puts up a fight. One of our men is hurt—or killed. Occasionally, one is caught and arrested. In that event, we want him taken care of decently. We want you to overlook the testimony of witnesses. We want to see the whole thing treated lightly so that the charges can be dismissed for lack of evidence, or, at worst, only a small fine will be imposed."

"So you have the judge in your pocket?"

"Indeed not. That would be dangerous and stupid. It is much safer for us to merely control the case before it reaches the judge. He's a rather stupid, but honest, man. He could be bought, I'm sure, but it is always risky to hire stupid people."

"That's my trouble; I'm pretty dumb," Beal said.

"Let's not be funny," Frame said. "You could do well for yourself in my organization. In a year, you could make five thousand dollars."

"While you make thirty thousand?"

Frame laughed. "Please, you're insulting my organization. The gross will be closer to a million. After expenses, four hundred thousand."

"And you run down the street and put that in the bank?" Beal asked.

"I take care of it," Frame admitted. "My offer is four hundred and fifty dollars a month."

"And if I say *no*?"

"You will be taken from this room and released in an alley behind the main street and will not be contacted again. However, you'll be marked. You won't live to cash your first pay check."

"I take it that's a promise."

"You can bet on it," Frame said.

"And if I say 'all right,' then what happens?"

"You'll go on salary immediately. Beal, you'll do your job, protect the decent, gentle people of Bonanza. In doing so, you'll even protect others, but the money paid to you by me is specifically to protect the men in my organization on occasions in which they cannot avoid trouble. You haven't much time to consider it."

"What have I got to consider? I'm dead if I don't agree." Beal shrugged. "All right, I'm your man. But I'll have to know who your men are and I want to see who I'm dealing with."

The marshal lunged out of the chair and across the table and crashed into the barred cage, stunning himself. He was picked up from the floor and placed in the chair again. There was a cut on his head which he felt gingerly.

Frame asked, "Have you learned anything, Mr. Beal?"

"Yeah, that you're smarter than me."

"No more trouble then?"

"No more," Beal said.

Chapter Three

June Collier sat up in bed. Her movement disturbed Adam; he was instantly awake.

She said, "Someone knocked on the door."

"At this hour?" He scratched a match and found that it was a quarter after three. Quickly, he slipped into his pants, lit the lamp, and went downstairs. As he moved along the hallway he could see the bulky shadow of a man on the other side of the frosted glass in the door. When he snapped back the lock and opened the door, Joe Beal ducked inside quickly.

"Put out that damned light, Adam. I'm sure I've been followed."

"What is it?"

Adam blew into the lamp chimney, and the two men stood in darkness.

"Were you home all evening?" Beal asked.

"Yes. After I left you, I came here and I haven't left the house."

Beal asked, "Your wife would swear to that?"

"If she had to," Collier told him. "What is this?"

"A little over two hours ago, two men I never saw before stuck a couple of guns in my ribs and took me to one of the houses on crib row. In a room somewhere in that house I met a nice fella who made me sit down with lamps shining in my face so I couldn't make him out." Beal leaned his shoulders against the door. "His voice sounded funny to me, hollow-like, but I think I've figured that out—he was talking from behind a water glass."

"You have no idea who it was?"

"No. I got the smart idea of jumping him, but he was sitting in a steel cage. All I got was a crack on my head." He fell silent for a moment. "Adam, I met the top man in Bonanza, the crime king himself. Your marshals that got killed were on the take. They were put out of the way because they tried to take too much."

"He told you this?"

"Yes. It is either work with him or get killed, and that could happen too easily, Adam. I was on the watch myself tonight, but I got braced just the same. But I've thought a few things out. First, why would a man want to disguise his voice?"

"To keep it from being recognized?"

"By me?" Beal shook his head. "I'm too new in town. The only voices I might recognize are yours, Enright's, Stiles, Madden, and Bridges. Oh, yes, there's Waller, and there's your friend who runs the Jackpot."

"That hadn't ought to be too hard to narrow down," Collier said.

"By me? I've been recruited, Adam. I can't nose around. Another thing: why would a man go to so much trouble to keep his identity a secret? I've known a lot of criminals who wouldn't stoop to pullin' on a mask." He tapped Collier on the chest. "The reason, I figure, is that everyone knows him. And not for what he really is."

"That makes sense. How are they goin' to use you?"

"To help cover up their trouble, when they get into it," Beal said. "They identify each other by sticking matches in the bands of their hats."

"So do a lot of people to cure a headache."

"Sure, but figure out the odds; they're in the favor of the toughs. Let's say there are twenty men in town with matches in their hatbands to cure a headache. These men are honest and don't want to get into trouble. So what does it hurt if they wear matches in their hatband? If a man is beaten and robbed and a tough gets tangled up in it and I arrest him, it's up to me to make sure the witnesses are never questioned too closely so that when the case gets to Judge Waller, it's a small fine or ten days in jail. Do you see how it is?"

"And you get paid to take care of the toughs?"

"Right. It's money well spent. A real ace in the hole."

"Come on in the parlor and sit down," Collier suggested. He led the way so Beal wouldn't stumble over any furniture. "Could you find the house again?"

"Yes, but I was told that it wouldn't do any good. The room was cleaned out after I left."

"That cage won't be easy to move."

"It's probably bolted together and comes apart easily," Beal said.

Collier grunted softly. "Joe, let this thing ride. I might be able to find out something."

"You can get yourself shot if you're not careful."

"Why would anyone want to shoot a fireman?" Adam got up and accompanied Beal to the door. "Make your rounds. I'll contact you in some way in a few days. And be damned careful."

"My intention," Beal said and left the house.

Collier went back upstairs and found his wife awake. He got in bed and pulled up the covers.

"One of the men from the firehouse," he explained. "Go to sleep."

"Funny it couldn't wait until morning," she said as she snuggled against him.

At six o'clock Adam had had his breakfast and was on his way to the firehouse on Pass Street. The relief was changing; he spent a few minutes talking to the men, then went into his small office and looked over the reports for the past twenty-four hours. An idea began to grow, and at eight-thirty he left the firehouse and walked along the main street until he came to the bank. Jim Enright was there, although he was not open for business; however, when Collier knocked, Enright came and opened the door.

"Putting in or taking out?" Enright asked and laughed at his own joke.

"Just something I want to talk over with you," Collier said. "Three months ago, you told me I could go ahead with my program to clean up the alleys and get rid of some of the fire hazards in town. Well, we haven't had a fire in sixty days that cost more than a hundred dollars in property damage. I'd like to go a little farther now."

"How far?"

"House-to-house inspection. Every building, every room, in the business district."

"But the owners will kick about that."

"I'm trying to protect them," Collier pointed out. "A bad fire could wipe out the whole street. They've got to see that."

"And how do you suppose I can get them to permit an inspection?"

"Let me write an article that Meers can publish in his paper. It's a very progressive step, your honor. Something you can talk about with pride at election time."

"Maybe you're right," Enright said. "All right, Adam. Go ahead."

At Clyde Meers' newspaper office, Collier found the publisher swearing at his printer's devil.

Meers said, "Just what I needed, an excuse to stop and have a drink. Ah, my boy, step into my study. Here, let me brush some of the debris off that chair. A pity how things accumulate no matter how tidy a man's natural instincts are. Just pile the papers on the floor. There." He got a bottle out of his littered desk and poured. "Now let me see, you wish to give me some local news? Insert an ad? You have something to sell?"

"I want to write an article for your paper and I thought you could give me some help with it."

"You've come to the right man," Meers admitted, bowing. "I do have a certain flair with words, even the ones we don't repeat in the presence of ladies. What is your subject?"

"Fire prevention."

"Nice subject. Dry, but still nice. And what is your proposal? Keep the buildings wet?" He waved his hand. "Pardon my sarcasm; I am never my jolly self until I'm half-drunk, and that does not occur until around eleven o'clock." He sat down on his desk and poured another drink for himself. "I have often thought a proper holocaust was just what this town needed and here I am, aiding and abetting the opposite. Ah, how fickle is man's sincerity!"

As soon as Collier finished at the newspaper

office, he walked back to the firehouse on Pass Street. His shift had the leather hoses laid out and were inspecting the stitching. The pumper was being washed down and fresh kindling laid in the firebox, ready for the match, ready to build up steam if the alarm bell rang. They were daily rituals, these minute inspections, for Collier felt that fire equipment must never fail; it could always happen at the wrong time.

Collier had a small office where he took care of his paper work, but, when there was none, he supervised the work. He was directing the inspection when a team and carriage pulled up the street and Roan Spencer ordered his driver to stop.

Spencer was a big man stuffed into a gray suit, in his mid-fifties, with the marks of his hard life clearly stamped in his face. He took the cigar from his mouth as Collier came over, and said, "Adam, I've got a boy working for me who thinks he can handle you. He's asked me to arrange it."

"The last two didn't work out too good for you, Roan. It would cost you another thousand dollars to find out."

Spencer laughed. "I'll tell you what I'll do, Adam. I think so much of this boy that I'll put up five thousand, winner take all."

Adam Collier took off his cap and scratched his head. "Now, that's a lot of money, Roan. You add that to my savings and the other two thousand you lost——"

"I think this boy of mine can do you in," Spencer said. "Damn it, someone in this gulch ought to be able to whip you. What do you say?"

"The usual rules?"

Spencer nodded. "A knockdown is a round. And the fight lasts until one of you can't toe the mark. You say the word and I'll set it up. This town needs some excitement."

"It does?" Collier laughed. "All right, Roan. You set it up. Say a week?"

"A week's fine," Spencer said. "Wait 'til you see this boy. He's strong."

The promoter tapped the driver on the shoulder and the rig wheeled around and went down the hill.

The firemen working outside had overheard the conversation. When Collier turned to go inside one of them asked, "Why do you do it, Adam?"

"Do you know an easier way to make five thousand dollars?"

"There must be safer ways," the man said. Then he grinned. "Your wife's going to raise hell again."

"Likely, she will."

"Well, you can always sleep here until she cools off," the man said.

"I may have to," Collier admitted.

He intended to go home in the middle of the afternoon, but the fire bell rang in the northwest corner of town and the station house turned into a riot of controlled confusion. The four-up team was wheeled into place and hitched to the pumper; the ladder wagon and hose wagons were already hitched, for the horses lived in harness. The engineer lit the paraffin-soaked shavings in the firebox. When the engine clanged out of the station, smoke belched from the flue as the driver—who had been discharged from the stagecoach company for recklessness—tore madly through the traffic. A slow-witted buggy driver failed to clear the way quickly enough and the rear hub of the pumper caught the smaller rig, flipping it neatly, and Collier, grimly hanging onto the back, turned in time to see Roan Spencer sitting in the street, shaking his fist after them and swearing. The rig was on its side, one wheel idly spinning, and the driver was trying to quiet the frightened horses.

The pumper rounded a corner, all wheels skidding while the rear of the heavy pumper slid into the boardwalk; the whirling iron rim ripped up a thirty-foot section, sending pieces of the walk flying. Collier closed his eyes and hung on, half tempted to fire the driver when they got back to the firehouse, and half tempted to praise him. He was the only driver who could reach a fire anywhere in town in five minutes flat.

The fire bell was still ringing. A man stood by the pole on the corner, frantically pulling on the rope. His house on a corner lot was belching smoke from the lower floors. The equipment arrived and the firemen pushed back the crowd. They took charge of the fire, dropping a hose and strainer into the man's well and starting the pumper, which throbbed and raced and belched smoke and steam with a furious noise. Three firemen grabbed the spouting hose nozzle and fearlessly pushed their way through the smoke into the house.

Collier walked over to the bell pole and told the man to stop the ringing. These poles were all over town, a system he had devised to speed the turning in of an alarm. The crowd thickened, but it did not hamper the firemen; a detail of four men was occupied just in keeping them out of the way of the fire fighters.

The man who had been ringing the fire bell remained still, his eyes round with shock. His eyebrows and half of his hair had been singed off and, from his reddening complexion, Collier knew that he would blister and peel.

"Suppose you tell me what happened?" Collier asked.

"I was hand-loading some shotgun shells and the powder ignited," the man said.

"Ignited from what?"

The man moved his head this way and that and looked at his house; there was the sound of glass breaking and wood splitting. "Do they have to wreck the place?"

"They won't damage anything they don't have to," Collier said. "You were going to tell me what started the fire."

"My cigar, I suppose. I thought it was out, so I tapped the end with my finger, you know, like you do to get rid of the ash before you light it again. Well, it wasn't out. I burned my finger, so I dropped it. I guess it fell in some loose powder."

"All right," Collier said. "You'd better go over and see Doc Stover. We'll put out the fire." He turned and saw Meers coming on the run.

"Hold on there!" Meers commanded, halting the man. He talked to him a moment, writing and nodding all the while, then he let the man go and came over to Adam Collier. "Getting the facts for the paper."

Smoke had stopped pouring out of the house and

one of the firemen came out, mopping grime and water from his face. He reported to Collier: "Most of the damage is confined to the kitchen. We've got the fire out. Now we're trying to mop it up a little. Quite a bit of smoke damage though."

"Let's have a look at it," Collier said. "Come along, Clyde." They crossed the lawn while firemen threw smoldering chunks of wood through an open window. Collier had his look at the kitchen; the walls were blackened by smoke and the reek of gunpowder was strong. The firemen were sweeping water out the back door and cleaning up some pieces of furniture that had been broken. Collier watched for a moment, then turned to the hall and stopped.

There was a small wooden settee there and a hall tree with a coat and hat hanging from it. He picked up the hat and pulled two matches from the band.

"He must suffer from headaches," Collier said.

"I don't put any stock in that," Meers admitted. "It's an old wives' tale."

"Yes, but it's interesting, nevertheless," Collier said. He put the matches back and rehung the hat. "Nothing more here. Got your story?"

"I can blow it up to a half a column," Meers said. "That's one of the advantages of being a good liar. Do you mind if I describe the heroic efforts of your firemen?" He laughed. "That was Roan Spencer's buggy your driver hit and upset on Gold Street. You could hear Roan cussing for two blocks."

"He'll be in to see me about it," Collier said absently. "And while you're wandering around, you might happen to run into the new marshal. Tell him to drop around to the firehouse the first chance he gets."

"What's going on?"

"Nothing." Collier smiled and went outside while his men started to fold the hoses and pack the equipment.

Chapter Four

Adam Collier did not go back to the fire station with the pumper and ladder rigs; instead, he walked four blocks over to Doctor Stover's office and found Stover reading a medical magazine.

Collier said, "With three doctors in a town this big, a man would think you'd have something else to do."

"Just boning up for the next case," Stover said. He was a few years older than Collier, in his mid-thirties, a well-built man with a shock of tawny hair and a resolute face.

"I sent you a patient," Collier said. "I'd like to talk to him." He saw Stover's blank look and went on. "A man in his forties. Most of his hair and eyebrows burned off."

"He didn't come here," Stover said. "Ah, yes, I heard the fire bell. No, he didn't show up here."

"I sent him here because you were closest," Collier said. "Funny. You'd think a man would——" Then he shrugged and smiled. "Well, I'll have to make the rounds, I guess."

"If he shows up, I'll tell him to go see you."

"If he shows up, you send someone around to get me." Collier picked up the magazine and dropped it in Stover's lap. "Learn. Be a good doctor."

"And you be careful with matches," Stover said.

Collier went back out to the street. Along Gold Street, ore wagons rumbled and gouged the earth and teamsters swore at the traffic, while, beyond town, the stamp mill pulsed and pounded and raised a vast cloud of dust that hung motionless in the still air.

Collier walked along, moving from side to side on the walk to take advantage of clear patches in pedestrian traffic. As he came abreast of the hotel, Roan Spencer's booming voice hailed him and Collier stepped onto the wide porch. Spencer was sitting in a rocking chair; he had a dark bruise on his cheekbone and one leg was stretched out stiffly in front of him.

"I ought to sue the city," Spencer said. "Adam, that damned driver is a maniac!" He flung his arms wide. "My rig's ruined. It'll take two weeks to repair. Now I ask you, what kind of an affair is this, when a man can't ride in his own rig down a main street without being run over by a fire engine?"

"It certainly does seem a shame, Roan," Collier admitted. "But it's surprising to me how a man will go to pot."

"Go to pot? Who's going to pot?"

Collier's shoulders rose and fell. "Well, I can recall the time when you could lick four men in a row and take a good bit of punishment doing it. Now, a little spill in the street——"

"Little spill? Why, the buggy flipped completely over! If I hadn't been a quick-witted, agile man and jumped clear, I'd likely have been crushed!" Spencer snorted indignantly and gnawed on his cigar. "It's all right for you to make light of this, Adam. You didn't get knocked around. But Enright's going to hear from me."

"While you're talking to him, see if you can't get the ore wagons off the main street. It won't hurt them to drive around town."

"Those are my wagons! Mine and Carlyle's. My drivers get paid by the trip, Adam. You know I want them to take the shortest route."

"It'll go a long way toward clearing the constant jam on Gold Street if you change the route," Collier pointed out. "I tell you this, Roan, because I know you're a considerate, thoughtful man, eager to better the community and the first to take hold——"

"Oh, for Christ's sake, don't spread it so thick," Spencer said. He rolled his shoulders and shifted his weight in the chair. "What am I, somebody's mother or something?" He sat there and looked at the moving press of mounted men and wagons slowly threading their great teams through. He listened to the din and brushed the constantly falling dust from his clothes. Then he said, "All right, I'll talk to Enright about an ordinance." He looked at Adam Collier. "Why aren't you in politics?"

"No interest."

"You always wanted to be a fireman—I know. A man with your talents—what a waste!" He pointed his cigar at Collier. "I want you to have a word with Hank Freely; a man just can't drive that way without killing someone sooner or later."

"I'll talk to Hank, for all the good it'll do," Collier promised. He started to step off the porch, then swung back. "Roan, you were in this country when it was nothing but heat, rattlesnakes, and Paiutes. You put up the first building here, you named the town. Look out there now and tell me how many people you know."

"They're mostly strangers to me," Spencer admitted. "It's the way a thing goes when a town booms. But a man still has his friends. I count you among my best, Adam. Always did." He frowned, pulling his bushy brows together. "I wish you'd pick your other friends with a bit more care."

"Referring to Bill Frame again?"

"I am," Spencer said flatly.

"What have you got against Bill? He never did a thing to you or said a word against you. Roan, sometimes I just don't figure you."

"This is a boom town," Spencer said, "and when I see a man running an honest game and serving uncut whiskey, then it just makes me mighty suspicious. Adam, I've been up and down the pike more times than I care to count. I've been in the meanest towns on earth and I'll tell you something: it was always a challenge to me, a game to be played, me against the crooks. Sometimes I managed to leave town with my poker winnings. Sometimes I had to fight and kill a man to keep what was mine. And there were times when I woke up in an alley with a cracked head and empty pockets. But I knew the risks, the rules, before I ever stepped into the play." He shook his head firmly. "No, an honest man just doesn't fit in that business. In yours, yes. In Meers', yes." He looked at Collier. "I guess I've said too much. A fault of mine."

"Anything you say is worth listening to," Collier said, "but I'm going to prove you wrong someday and, when I do, I'll expect you to go to Bill Frame and apologize."

"I'm not wrong," Spencer maintained.

Collier laughed in spite of his irritation. "Roan, you're a damned stubborn man."

"Ain't that a fact?"

Adam Collier sat at the head of the table; his daughter sat on his left, and the twin boys on his right. June Collier put the food on the table, setting each platter down a little sharply. Then she took her place at the other end, her expression prim and angry.

"Not just a little smile?" Collier coaxed.

"Now don't you start that, Adam. Oh, you vex me to tears!"

The little girl asked, "Are you going to cry, Mama?"

"Mash your potatoes and put on gravy, Sissy," June Collier said. "Boys, stop fussing and eat!" She picked up her knife and fork and gripped them until her knuckles were white.

"Is Papa going to fight again?" Sissy asked insistently.

"Oh, that does it!" June snapped. "When a seven-year-old child——"

"Mash your potatoes like your mother says."

"Every time I talk when I shouldn't," Sissy complained, "it's 'go wash your face' or 'go pick up your room.'"

"Sometimes you're even told to leave the table," Adam Collier said. "So let's do as we're told, huh?"

"I've made up my mind, Adam," June said. "You are not going to fight anyone."

"I told Spencer I would."

"Tell him you've changed your mind."

"Now I don't see how I can rightly do that. Besides, five thousand dollars——"

"We don't need the money. Adam, we have six

thousand dollars in the bank right now. Why, that's more than my father managed to save in a lifetime."

"The money is security for you and the children," he said. "That's all I considered when I told Spencer."

"Well, tell him you've reconsidered. Adam, I mean it. You are not going to fight!" June looked steadily at him. "Forgive me for saying this, but you drive me to it: if you fight this man, I'll take the children and——" She let her knife and fork clatter to the plate and put her hands over her face.

The children stared, stunned, Adam Collier said, "I'll tell Roan Spencer it's off, but I want you to understand something. June, look at me when I talk to you. I want you to understand that I'll call it off because I understand now how much you are against it, and not because you felt that you had to threaten me. I love you, June. Your happiness means more to me than, well—anyone else's opinion."

She got up with a rush and came around the table and nearly upset Adam when she sat on his lap and flung her arms around him.

The children giggled, and Adam snapped his fingers and said, "Eat," before she shut him up with a kiss.

The children squealed and the boys banged their forks on the table and June got off his lap and blushed, she clapped her hands and restored order before she sat down at her place.

"There's nothing like a peaceful meal in a man's own home," Collier said, smiling. "Take some peas, Tad. I know you don't like 'em, but that way you'll learn to eat 'em. If you try hard, you may grow up and find they're your favo—no, you don't think so? Well you eat some anyway."

Someone tapped on the kitchen door. Collier got up and let Joe Beal in.

Joe took off his hat and bowed to June. "Forgive the intrusion, but——"

"Won't you have something with us?" she asked.

"Thank you, ma'am; I've eaten. Adam, I couldn't get over to the firehouse, so I waited until it was dark to come here."

"Come on into the parlor," Collier said and led the way. He waved Beal into a chair that was hidden from view through the front windows. "We had a little fire this afternoon. I happened to notice the hat that belonged to the owner of the house. Matches in the hatband. I sent him to see Doc Stover because he'd been scorched a bit, but he never went there. You ought to be able to find him; his eyebrows and half his hair are gone, and he'll have water blisters on his face. Hands, too, probably."

"And if I find him?"

"Get his name, where he works, all you can about him. Tell him it's for the fire report."

"All right," Beal said. He got up and went into the kitchen. "Sorry I disturbed you. Good night." Collier closed the door after him and sat down at the table.

"Just a little business I wanted the marshal to look into," Collier said. The newspaper thudded onto his front porch and all the children yelled: "I'll get it!" as they bounded out of their chairs. They tried to get through the doorway together and upset themselves. While they were tangled on the floor, Collier stepped over them and got his paper.

When he came back to the table, he said, "I will never be able to understand why the boy can't deliver it before my supper or immediately after."

He opened the paper, glanced at the front page, and his attention gravitated to an article near the bottom.

"Roan Spencer didn't waste any time," he said, handing the paper to his wife. June read the lead line:

FIRE CHIEF ACCEPTS CHALLENGE

He watched her eyes dart over the paragraph, then he said, "I gave you my word, June. The matter's settled. Spencer can call it off."

"That won't be easy now, will it?"

He shook his head.

"I've got you into something, haven't I?"

"No, I got myself into it for moving too quickly. I'll work it out, June. Now let's not talk about it."

While his wife cleaned off the table and washed the dishes, Collier read a story to his children and shooed them upstairs to bed. He smoked a cigar; then he went up to tuck them in and settle their last disputes of the day.

Finally, he settled down with his paper and cigar, a contented, domesticated man, disturbed only by the thought that he would have to see Roan Spencer in the morning. Spencer would listen and give Collier his way, but it wouldn't be a good thing, and this worried Adam Collier.

At the firehouse the next morning, Collier heard that two men had been found dead in the alley back of Gold Street. They had been beaten to death and robbed and it was common knowledge that they had been big winners in the games along the street.

Apparently, no one had witnessed the killings, and, like the other times, everyone was in an uproar about it, insisting that something just had to be done to clean up Bonanza. Enright's office, Collier knew, would be full of indignant citizens, the good citizens who had become indignant over a lot of things, and the next town board meeting would be a lively one.

Collier still had Roan Spencer in mind as he went to the barn in back of the firehouse and saddled his horse. He rode four miles out of town to the Occidental mine.

The mine was well up the flank of a bare mountain. The ore wagons, governed by signal flags, traveled up and down a treacherous winding road which led to it. Before starting down, a wagon driver would look at the signal at the bottom, and if it were flying, he would wait for the empty which was coming up the one-way track. At the bottom, the drivers checked the flag at the top in the same way to see if the track were clear. The loaded ore wagons rolled rapidly down the grade, brake blocks smoking against their iron rims to control them, and the empty wagons ground slowly up the grade.

Spencer's buildings, bunkhouses, cookhouse, stable, and stable yard were in a huge compound at the base of the mountain. Collier's destination was the miner's office, which was the main building in the group.

Collier rode up to the office, tied up, and went inside. He found Spencer at his desk, a bit surprised to find out who his visitor was.

"Have a cigar and sit down, Adam," Spencer said.

"You may want to throw me out," Collier said. "Roan, I've changed my mind about the fight."

"But you can't do that!"

"Already have. I'm sorry, but that's the way it is."

"But it's in the paper."

"I saw it. It's off."

Spencer spent a moment licking and lighting a cigar. "Adam, I never knew you to go back on a deal. This isn't going to be easy to explain, you know."

"I'm not going to explain it, Roan."

"You know how the talk will go?"

"There's only one way. Let it. The men in this town who matter know me well enough not to believe it."

Spencer drew on his cigar. "I really have a big boy this time, Adam. He's not much of a scientific fighter like you are. You know, never was captain of a boxing team or anything like that. But he's strong—a real bruiser who's crippled a few in his time. What I'm trying to say is that folks are going to look at him and then say you had a look and got cold feet. I know that isn't so. You've got your reasons and they're good enough for me. But what about the others?"

"They can go to hell," Collier said. "I hate to take that attitude with you, Roan, but I'm not going to fight him. I'm sorry now I ever took on the first one."

"It was just sport," Spencer said. "Hell, you used to fight in the army: best man in the company against best man in another company."

"And I think now that it was a lot of damned foolishness. Some good men got marked pretty badly because of it."

"It's the way men are, Adam. Hell, life's rough." Roan sighed and waved his hands. "All right, I'm not trying to argue with you, persuade you. All right, the deal's off. But I'm disappointed."

"No hard feelings?"

"No, just disappointed. If you change your mind, Adam——"

"I don't think I'll do that," Collier said. He opened his mouth to say something more, then closed it.

Roan Spencer said, "Adam, was it June that raised hell?" He waited a moment. "I don't blame her, really, and this is between you and me; it'll never go any farther."

"I don't think it's worth talking about, Roan."

"Sure, sure," Spencer said. "I used to back down for my wife, bless her memory, and it never was because I had to. I did it because I loved the ground she walked on."

"You're a good friend, Roan," Collier said. "And an understanding one."

"Sure, but a lot of good that'll do you when the word gets around."

Chapter Five

When Adam Collier, in the company of three fire-men, began his systematic inspection of the commercial buildings along Gold Street, he met no resistance from the merchants because they wanted to prevent fires and were willing to clean up or correct any hazards Collier found. Some of the saloon owners complained, but Collier kept his temper and convinced them that this method was the best thing and his men inspected the buildings from top to bottom.

This was not a job to be done in a day; it took him four days to work from one end of the street to the other. A few wagonloads of trash were hauled away and, in the end, the buildings were safer than before, but he had found nothing important to tell Joe Beal about.

They met openly on the street or in stores as though they had bumped into each other and stopped to talk. Beal had made no progress on the two robberies and the matter hung fire, another unsolved crime.

When the newspaper came out there was a piece in it about the fight being called off. This caused men to talk although no one came up to Adam Collier and asked him about it.

Collier was about to go off duty one day when Beal dropped around at the firehouse; they went outside and tipped their chairs against the wall and talked as though they were passing the time of day.

"I've worked up an idea," Beal said, "but I'll need help on it." He took his pocketknife from his pocket and began whittling. "I know a man in San Francisco, a professional gambler. He'd come here if I asked him to. He could drift into town, dressed like he'd just come from the diggings. In one night, Adam, he could clean out a place."

"And then?"

"It's the big winners that attract these toughs. All right, he wins and gets out and ducks into an alley. I'll be there waiting for him. You'll be a little farther down where you can follow me. I'll change clothes with him so they'll jump me. They'll take the bait. Only I'll be armed and waiting for 'em."

"That sounds like the hard way to get a couple of toughs."

"We might get lucky, Adam. One of these times, we're going to recognize one as someone we've seen around town. And maybe then we'll remember who we saw him with. You see how a chain could build?"

Collier nodded. "No matter what turned up, we'd be better off than now. Go ahead and send for your man."

"Already did," Beal admitted. "He ought to arrive in a week or two. I'll point him out to you." He folded his knife and got up. "I'll walk around. That's what I get paid to do. But I'd like to slap someone in the jail who was more than a drunk raising hell."

"You don't suppose you could be going at this from the wrong end, do you?"

"What do you mean?"

"The total lifted off these men must come to a big bagful. Or more like a wagonload. Is it put in the bank? What happens to it? Buried in the ground?" Collier shook his head. "It's all specie, Joe, so it's either melted down at the assayer's or the smelter, or it is salted away. It ought to be looked into."

"Let me try my way," Beal suggested.

"All right. You're the marshal."

After Beal went down the street, Collier made a final tour of the firehouse. Then he started home, his tin lunch bucket under his arm. Gold Street was jammed with traffic; the walks were so crowded that he had to elbow his way along. As he passed the Jackpot, he heard someone calling him and looked around. Bill Frame was on the porch, waving his arm so Collier veered toward the steps, pushing his way through the men.

"Payday at the Occidental," Frame said. "Have a drink before you go home."

Collier consulted his watch. "Can't stay long. June has supper waiting."

"A short one," Frame insisted, taking his arm and steering him inside.

The place was a press of men. They worked their way to the back and entered Frame's office. He closed the door and poured two drinks.

"You're not hurting for business," Collier said. "I'm glad to see you make it, Bill."

"I think you are," Frame said. He sat down and tipped back his chair. "We were strange bedfellows, Adam. But I've always been glad to have you as a friend. The rich boy and the poor boy. There's something classic about that."

Collier frowned. "Not rich, Bill. My father was just a druggist, nothing more."

"Rich compared to me," Frame said. "But the Academy made us all equal, didn't it, Adam? You put on that blue suit and no one can tell the difference. Right."

"If that's what you want it to do, it'll do it," Collier admitted.

"Doesn't anything bother you?"

"Why let it?" Collier asked. "What should bother me, Bill?"

"Adam, what the hell are you doing working as fire chief?"

"It's a good job. I like being a fireman. There's more to it than meets the eye, Bill."

"Agh!" He waved his hand. "You're a fool, Adam. A man with your brains could be rich in a year. Me, I like to sleep in a silk nightshirt and smoke ten-cent cigars."

"If I had a lot of money, what would I do with it?" Collier asked. He turned his head when a knock rattled the door.

"It's open," Frame said.

The door swung wide and a huge man stood there. He had a round head that seemed to be joined directly with his shoulders; his neck was extremely short and thick. He looked at Collier and said, "You must be the fireman."

"Why, are you on fire?"

"I hear you don't want to fight me."

"So you're the one." Collier shook his head. "You'll have to find someone else to fight."

"I picked you," the man said. He looked around

the room and saw the other door. "I'm goin' back to the bar and I'll wait there, and if you ain't scared of me, you'll leave through the front door."

"You're wasting your time," Collier said evenly.

"We'll see," the man said and backed out, closing the door.

Bill Frame blew out a long breath. "Now he's a big one. Hands the size of a scoop shovel. His name's Malloy and he's a rough one, Adam. You can go out the back way if you want."

"Thanks, no." Adam looked at his watch. "Just time for me to get home to supper. Thanks for the drink, Bill." He got up and walked to the door. "Save your money, huh?" He smiled and stepped out.

He had no doubts how things were going to be. He had hardly entered the main bar and gambling room when men stepped back to let him pass through. They were set for this, waiting for it, and, at the bar, Malloy turned and looked at Collier.

The noise died down as though a huge pillow had been shoved over the entire place.

Malloy laughed and said, "I kind of expected you to come this way, fireman."

Malloy moved away from the bar and the crowd remained solidly packed; they had no intention of letting Collier through until Malloy's challenge was met.

"You wouldn't want a man to be late for supper now would you, Malloy?"

"Fireman, when we're through, you'll be on mashed potatoes and milk for a month." Malloy peeled off his shirt and threw it backward, then he dropped his suspenders and rolled up the sleeves of his flannel underwear. He had arms like ash boles, heavy with hair, and his blunt face broke into a handsome, pleased smile.

"Now do you want to stomp your feet a couple of times, Fireman, just to get into the swing of it, or do we dance this one cold?"

Collier shook his head negatively and let his glance casually take in the area surrounding him. A poker table near him had been hastily vacated, but he was hemmed in by tables and chairs because Bill Frame couldn't bear to waste a little space if there was a dollar to be made.

"Then I guess I'll come to you," Malloy said. He bulled forward, his boots stirring the soiled sawdust. He was like a rushing ore wagon which had broken loose going down a long grade; once started, he was nearly impossible to stop.

Collier snatched up a chair and swung it low, catching Malloy across the ankles and shins, spilling him headlong. His falling weight demolished two chairs and sheered the leg completely off a poker table; chips and specie were flung into the air and cards scattered wildly. Men scrambled for the money and Malloy lay on the floor, clutching his legs.

"I'll get up," he said. "Give me time and I'll get up."

"Some other time," Collier said dryly and roughly pushed his way out of the place.

Walking home, Collier felt a rising irritation, not against Malloy, but at mankind in general; they liked trouble better than anything as long as it was not turned on themselves.

The children were waiting at the gate for him and he hoisted the girl to his shoulders and walked on to the porch with the boys clinging to his legs. June opened the door for him and kissed him. "I made chicken pie, Adam. One of the ranchers from the basin came by this afternoon and he had these spring chickens and some early peas—so we're not going to have pot roast after all. Mind?"

"I'm just glad I'm not late," he said as he put his arm around her and walked with her to the kitchen.

June had the table set. Everyone took their places and June said grace. Then the family put napkins in their laps and the pie was passed around. She was full of woman talk and Adam listened to her carefully; she heard the opinion of wives and wives had influence on their husbands; it was this barometer that gave Collier the edge on other men when it came to predicting the turn of events. The wives and mothers had wanted a bigger school in Bonanza; the town board had another opinion; they thought the school was adequate and would not consider spending the money. Collier gambled that there would be a new school and pushed for it because the women were in a snit and, although a man could tell a woman to shut her mouth on a given subject and be obeyed, he couldn't abide burned eggs in the morning or a cold shoulder in bed at night.

Not for long anyway.

June was talking about how dusty the walks were in the summer and how dangerous the dried-out loose boards were, and how slippery they became in the winter, and Adam Collier filed it in the back of his mind that there would likely be cement walks laid along Gold Street before spring.

June interrupted herself and said, "My, it sure is noisy tonight. Are they tearing up Gold Street?"

This drew Collier's attention to the fact that there was an unusual amount of hubbub which seemed to be getting louder: men yelling and cheering and the dull throb of many boots marching on the street. The noise rose to a crescendo in front of his house. He threw aside his napkin and got up to see what the disturbance was all about. He opened the front door and saw several hundred men blocking the street. Malloy was there, his young face split by a wide grin. Two men that Collier recognized ripped his front gate off the hinges and followed Malloy to the porch.

June and the children had come to the door and crowded around Collier.

June shouted: "Look what you've done to my gate! I know you, Jake Powell. You'll fix my gate!"

Collier put his hand on June's arm and she fell silent, still furious. "This is Mr. Malloy," he explained to her. "He wants to fight."

"Well, go somewhere else and fight!" she snapped.

The two men behind Malloy, the Powell brothers, laughed and Jake said, "Adam, you wouldn't be hiding behind a woman now, would you?"

"I'm going to see you about fixing my gate," Collier said civilly.

"I'll do it when hell freezes over," Jake said. He nudged his brother. "Ain't that right, BooBoo?"

"It surely is."

They slapped their legs and laughed. Then Jake showed Collier the rock he had been carrying—he drew back his arm and threw it through the parlor window.

"You goin' to make us fix that too?" he taunted.

The crowd was silent. Malloy said, "Fireman, you can't get out of this."

"*Now*, I don't want to," Collier said. He took off his brass-buttoned coat; he handed it to his wife. "Malloy, I'm going to give you your fight because you're standing between me and the Powell boys."

"If you're going to fight," June said hotly, "then you lick him good, Adam."

Malloy continued to smile and the Powell boys thought this was hilarious. Collier stepped off the porch and Malloy decided not to wait any longer; he swung from way down, starting the punch slow as though he wanted to aim it accurately. Collier ducked it and jabbed with his left—a solid, well-timed punch with a hundred-and-eighty-five pounds of trained muscle behind it. He smashed Malloy's nose and snapped his head back, driving him off balance so that he had to take two backward steps to keep from falling.

As his blood started to flow, Malloy's eyes got round with surprise; there was no pain, not now, but in an hour it would be shooting through his head like hot pokers.

But there was no fear in the man; he came at Collier, stamping his huge feet, flailing his arms. Collier simply let him close in, then he squatted, and let Malloy fan the air. He came up on the side and cocked a punch, snapped it out, and caught Malloy on the side of the jaw. It was short and hard and Malloy, in spite of his bulk and weight, was spun completely around. He fell heavily, rolling on the ground to get away from any kick aimed at him.

The Powell brothers looked at Malloy as he got up.

Jake said, "Well, for Christ's sake, hit him! He ain't no shadow, you know."

"I'll get him," Malloy said and wiped his hands on his pants. Blood was streaming from his nose and there was a dark red mark on his jaw where Collier had struck him.

"You'd better send your woman and kids inside, Fireman. I'm goin' to hurt you now," Malloy gibed.

He sprang up like a track star leaving the mark and came at Collier, both arms outflung, meaning to grapple him. Collier let him grab, but, as soon as the brawny arms went around him, he laced his fingers and brought the back edge of his hands down against Malloy's neck.

The savage blow wrung a deep grunt from Malloy and his body seemed to turn to rubber; he sagged to his knees. Collier stepped back and let him fall on his face.

The Powell brothers were dancing about excitedly. "Get up! Get up!"

"Leave him alone," Collier said. He stood above his opponent, waiting and Malloy rolled slowly over on his back, his breathing heavy, the air bubbling in his smashed nose. "You've had enough, Malloy. Let it go now."

Malloy kept shaking his head and Marshal Joe Beal rammed his way through the crowd. He looked at Malloy, then at Adam Collier and said, "I'll arrest the whole lot if you'll sign the complaint, Adam."

"It's nothing I can't take care of," Collier said.

"We're waiting for Mr. Malloy to get up so he can have the fight he wanted so bad." He swung his glance to the Powell brothers. "Then I'm coming after you two."

Chapter Six

There wasn't a man there who couldn't see that Malloy had already had enough, but he had to get up, he had to put on the show for them or be through in the camp. And there wasn't a man present who thought he could beat Adam Collier; before, there had been hope, but that was gone now.

Malloy got up and was unsteady for a moment, then he said, "Let's get it over with, Fireman."

"You don't owe these men anything," Collier said.

"Don't I?" Malloy tried to smile, then he shook his head. "It's turned around now, ain't it? I have to go through with it just like I made you go through with it."

"Why don't you come into my house?" Collier invited. "June, take Mr. Malloy into the parlor and get him a drink and put a cold cloth on his nose."

June went down off the porch and touched his arm; he towered over her; yet, when she guided him toward the porch, he followed without protest. Collier turned and looked at Jake and BooBoo Powell and they suddenly realized their danger, they turned and tried to bolt, but the men behind them caught them and flung them back—the same men who had, moments before, followed them and cheered them on.

With nowhere to go, Jake decided to make a stand.

"We can lick him, BooBoo!" Jake cried and came in toward Collier swinging.

Collier let Jake's fist bounce off his shoulder, then he grabbed Jake around the neck and hit him four times in the nose and eyes before turning him loose.

BooBoo shoved the crowd aside frantically and ran, dashing across the yard and jumping the fence; he caught his coat and ripped it but this hardly slowed him down. He ran rapidly up the street and disappeared.

Everyone laughed except his brother and Adam Collier.

Jake was sitting on the lawn, bleeding, pressing his hands to his face. "I've had enough! I've had enough!" he cried.

"That's the second time you've tried to do me in," Collier said. "The third time, they may hold a funeral for you two."

Joe Beal's attention sharpened. "What's this?"

"Jake and BooBoo tried to run me down with their horses one night," Collier said. "I really didn't recognize them at the time, but seeing them again, I know it was them." He reached down, fisted a handful of Jake's coat, and hauled him up. "You trying to get even, Jake?"

"No, no, it wasn't anything like that!"

"Today, you'll build me a new gate and paint it. You find BooBoo and tell him to get a new glass for my window and put it in."

"I'll see that they do it," Beal said. "Now, you people get the hell out of this man's yard before I run you in for trespassing."

Collier turned and went into his house. Malloy was sitting in the parlor, his head tipped back; June had a pan of water and a cloth and was trying to repair some of the damage around his broken nose. The children stood in the hallway, not sure they should be there, but determined to stay until told to leave.

"Sissy," Collier said, "you run over to Doc Stover's house and tell him to come right away. Tell him we need his help."

"Yes, papa." She dashed out of the house, slamming the door behind her.

Collier stepped into the parlor, standing to one side so his wife could work undisturbed, yet where he could see Malloy.

"Fireman," Malloy said through the damp folds of cloth, "I'd have stomped your ribs loose if I could."

"I know the rules," Collier said. "Do you want a drink?"

Malloy shook his head. "You knew you could lick me, didn't you?"

"I rather thought I could," Collier said. He drew up a chair and sat down. "Malloy, when I was at the United States Military Academy at West Point, I trained under an Englishman who was the boxing champion of Europe. He'd fought fifty-one times and had never been knocked to his knees. There were no more than three scars on his face. I thought he was a fine gentleman because he never wanted to fight any man unless he was absolutely forced to. You did that to me, Malloy. I didn't want to fight you. I hurt you because it was the only way I could stop you."

"Any man can be licked," Malloy said. "I always believed that."

"That's right, if a man's stupid enough to fight 'em all. I try not to be that dumb." He reached over and put his arm around his wife. "Kind of got your blood up out there, didn't you, old girl?"

"Now don't you rub it in, Adam Collier."

Sissy's clatter on the porch preceded the doctor by three minutes. Doc Stover came in, put June aside gently and examined Malloy's nose.

"You did a good job, as usual, Adam," the doctor said. "Is it all right if I work right here? . . . Thank you, then perhaps you'd get me some towels, June."

The children were again blocking the archway and Collier shooed them toward their bedrooms.

"But I want to watch, Papa," Sissy said.

"Now you've had your excitement and done your good deed for today, so why spoil it by making your father yell at you?" Adam gave her a playful smack on the bottom, and herded all three children to their rooms.

Dinner was cold, so Adam poured some coffee and was drinking it when June came in, went to him silently, and put her arms around him. "My chicken pie—and I was so proud of it."

"Can't you reheat it?"

"Oh, you don't know anything about cooking. It's no good heated over."

"Can't we pretend that it is?"

June looked at him and smiled, letting her smile grow until she was laughing. Then she put some wood in the stove and began to heat the oven.

Doc Stover came into the kitchen a little while later searching for a match so he could light his pipe.

"I gave Malloy some powders to dull the pain," he said. "Are you going to let him perch on your couch all night? To my way of thinking, that's carrying hospitality a little too far."

"You want me to throw him out in the street?" Collier asked.

"No, I suppose not." He helped himself to coffee, then he saw the chicken pie. "Ah, cold chicken pie! What a delicacy. Surely you don't mind—thank you, June, you're a woman after my own heart." He sat down and began to eat.

Collier watched him a moment, then said, "Well, I suppose that's how man discovered fire. Want some cold chicken pie, June?"

"You are both completely out of your minds," she said and put the rest of the pie in the oven to heat.

"Let me ask you an academic question, Adam," Stover said. "From a medical point of view, how do you hit a man so hard and not damage your hands? I've dealt with a few smashed knuckles in my day so I'd like to know."

"It would take you a couple of years to learn," Collier said. "A bare-knuckle fighter who can't take care of his hands is in trouble. He could hit a man a solid lick once only, then he'd be through."

"I'd like to have hit that Jake Powell with a skillet," June said. "The idea—tearing up my gate and breaking my parlor window."

"This fellow, Malloy—wasn't he the one Roan Spencer had lined up to fight you?" Stover asked. He laughed. "Roan's no fool, you know. He'd throw out a few thousand, betting on Malloy, then quietly have his men take ten or fifteen thousand on you. If he didn't come out to the good on these things, I'll miss my guess."

"That sounds almost crooked."

"It sounds like a safe way to make money," Stover said. "Pitting a bruiser against a trained fighter. It would be like sending a six-fingered kid with dropsy up against John Wesley Hardin. Yet there are men who'll bet on the off-chance that Hardin would miss, or that you'd get caught by a lucky punch." He sighed and finished his pie, then wiped his lips on the napkin. "Delicious, simply delicious, June. If you ever plan to take in a boarder, by all means notify me."

"You're a fraud, Doctor Stover," June said. "I don't think you ever really went to medical school at all."

"Ah, discovered!" Stover exclaimed. "I knew it would come out someday. The next baby you have, you will find my fee increased to seventy-five dollars." He clapped on his hat and locked his pipe between his teeth. "When Mr. Malloy comes round, tell him he owes me four dollars, and warn him that I hound my patients to death when they don't pay."

Collier walked him to the door, saw him out, then he stopped in the parlor and looked at Malloy. The huge man was sleeping, his face heavily bandaged; two bamboo sticks, which protruded from the windings, held his nose in position while it healed.

It was dark when Joe Beal came back with the Powell brothers; they had tools and wood and Boo-Boo gingerly carried a large sheet of glass. They worked for over an hour by lanternlight, repairing the gate and window. Adam Collier sat on his front porch and watched them, enjoying the evening breeze and his cigar.

The fence was finally painted and the window carefully puttied before the Powell brothers were allowed to go. Beal came to the porch and stood there in the darkness, his cigar end glowing and dying as he puffed on it.

"Your wife around?"

"She was tired and went upstairs to lie down. The kids are sound asleep."

"I'm expecting my friend on next week's stage."

"Good. I'll be ready when you are."

"You think these Powell boys are part of the gang of toughs?"

"They're not very tough," Collier said.

"How tough does a man have to be to sneak around in the dark with a stick of lead in his hand, or a gun?"

"That's a good point," Collier admitted. "What do you think of Malloy?"

"You mean, is he a part of the crew? I'd say *no*. Just a guess, but I'd bet on it. Malloy isn't the type. He faces a man. He's strong and proud of it. No, no, not Malloy. You couldn't pay him to take a man from behind in a dark alley."

"Have you had any other contact with the man in the cage?"

"Nope. No one's said a word to me. I've got the jail half full of riffraff and Enright thinks I'm doing a great job." He laughed humorlessly. "Well, I've got rounds to make. I'll keep in touch." He shied his cigar onto the lawn and walked to the street where he jumped over the picket fence rather than use the newly painted gate.

* * *

Bill Frame left his place, the Jackpot, shortly before nine, got his horse from the stable, saddled, and rode out to the Occidental mine. He tied up in front of the main building and went into Roan Spencer's office.

"You're early," Spencer said. "Fred and the others won't be here for another thirty minutes."

"I don't mind waiting a half hour for a big-stake game," Frame said. "I suppose you heard about your friend, Malloy."

Spencer's eyebrows went up. "No, what about him?"

"He braced Collier in my place, then later went to Collier's house. He ended up on the ground—badly battered, I hear."

"I'll be damned! He was a big fella. Strong, too." Spencer shook his head. "What does it take to whip that man Collier?"

"Someone weighing two-hundred pounds who's fought professionally and is as quick as a cat," Frame said. He turned as Jim Enright came in. "You're early, Jim."

"So I see. You could have come out with me in the buggy, Bill." He pushed the tails of his coat aside and sat down, rubbing his hands. "I can feel Lady Luck sitting on my shoulders tonight."

Spencer laughed. "As soon as Fred Carlyle gets here, we'll find out. But you'll need gold to back that luck, Jim."

"I've got it," Enright said and sat back to enjoy his cigar.

Fred Carlyle arrived a few minutes late—a tall, thin man in his middle fifties dressed in an expensive suit, wearing a locomotive headlight diamond in his ascot. He looked like a wealthy mining man and there was a bit of rivalry between Carlyle and Spencer to see which of them could take the most ore from the ground.

The game was stud, played in silence amid thick cigar smoke; the rattle of money was the only sound, for the men played seriously, with the door locked, and a fortune on the table.

By midnight, every man knew that Jim Enright's hunch about his luck was no joke. They changed decks often, changed the deal often, but Enright played his cards and he kept getting the cards and the money, until by a quarter after one he had nearly thirty thousand dollars, most of it contributed by Spencer and Carlyle, who not only could afford to lose it, but just could not resist calling.

Frame had dropped over six thousand. The game had turned off three-handed and no one seemed to notice or care that he had dropped out. At two o'clock he got up, quitting the game. He said good night and went out to stand by his horse. He lit a cigar and, from his pocket, he took three small pieces of paper, each with a name written on it: Enright, Carlyle, and Spencer. The ones with "Spencer" and "Carlyle" he put in his mouth and chewed to a soggy nothing; then he spit the wad out, mounted, and rode back toward town.

Halfway up the long climb to the town, he began to whistle and, a moment later, he heard an answering signal. Frame struck a match but held it away from him so that he would not be seen, dropped the paper, and rode on. When he was nearly out of sight, BooBoo Powell and his brother came from the brush near the side of the road, picked up the paper, and peered at the name.

"Enright," Jake said. "We'll get him here."

They waited for nearly an hour, then they heard the buggy coming. Finally, they saw it; they let it pass then jumped the rig. Enright was taken by surprise and tried to throw up his hands, but BooBoo crashed a lead stick down across the base of his skull, while Jake pulled the team up. Enright fell out of the buggy. BooBoo pounced on him and hit him twice more. Jake heard the sound of the lead crushing Enright's skull and jumped down, pushing BooBoo back. He bent then and felt for Enright's heartbeat.

"For Christ's sake, you killed him! You damned fool, I told you one lick was enough, and not too hard either." Jake grabbed BooBoo by the arm. "Get our horses. I'll get the money."

He found the loot under the buggy seat in a leather satchel, then he lifted Enright, put him alongside the road, gave the team a smart slap and sent them on to town, knowing they'd return to the stable.

BooBoo came up with the riding horses and Jake mounted.

BooBoo whined, "Well, we got the money, didn't we? Ain't that all that mattered?"

"Aw, shut up, will you?" Jake gigged his horse and stormed away, BooBoo following, still protesting that he was being treated unfairly.

Chapter Seven

Pete Madden came to Adam Collier's house while he was having his breakfast; he knocked at the back door and came in without waiting for a welcome.

"Adam, I've got some bad news. Jim Enright was killed sometime late last night. Out on the Occidental mine road." He looked apologetically at June and the children. "Jeff Stiles has called a town council meeting this morning."

"What time?"

"Now," Madden said. "They sent me to get you."

"All right," Collier said. "I'll be right along." He put down his coffee cup and napkin and got up. "Any idea how it happened, or who did it?"

"Robbery, that's all I heard. I'll see you in the courthouse, Adam." He clapped on his hat and went out, letting the back door slam.

Collier got his coat and hat and kissed June. "I don't know when I'll be home now," he said. "If it's late I'll try and send someone around to let you know."

"I'll go over to Mrs. Enright's as soon as I can," she said.

He nodded and went out the front way, walking rapidly toward the center of town. Crossing the streets he ducked the traffic and went into the courthouse.

As he approached the board room, he could hear talk, but it stopped when he stepped inside. Joe Beal was there, and the rest of the council was present, waiting for him.

Collier said, "I'm sorry to be late, but Pete just——"

"Yes, we know," Jeff Stiles said. "This is a terrible thing, Adam. We were just talking about it."

Collier looked at Joe Beal. "What did you find out?"

"That he played high-stake poker last night with Roan Spencer, Fred Carlyle, and Bill Frame. Jim won the big share. Frame checked out of the game and came back to town. Jim left the game sometime after that in his buggy. He was jumped about a mile and a half from the mine. Two men."

"How can you tell?" Stiles asked.

"Tracks. They robbed him, sent the team on into town, and left him lyin' in the road. Dead. Then they mounted up and rode back to town." He waved his hand to indicate Gold Street. "They're out there somewhere, walkin' around, a part of the crowd."

"It's obvious to us," Howard Bridges said, "that Jim was robbed and killed in the process of the robbery. But that's a matter for the marshal to investigate. Right now, we're without a mayor."

"The reason we're here ahead of you," Pete Madden admitted, "is because we wanted to talk this over before you got here."

"Talk what over?" Collier asked.

"We want you to take Jim Enright's place," Stiles said. "It's in our power to appoint a mayor until next election, and that's over two years away. We all agree to this, Adam. You're the only man for the job."

"That certainly is flattering."

"We've also decided that you were right all along," Stiles said. "This town has to be cleaned up, not just on the surface, the drunks and fist fights, but cleaned out from top to bottom so that when we're through there won't be a tough left."

Collier looked at them solemnly. "Now, I've asked that we clean up Bonanza for some time, but you were always afraid for your wives and families. The danger may be even worse today."

"We know that," Madden said flatly. "But we've made up our minds, Adam. Will you sit in Jim's chair?"

"If I do, gentlemen, I'm going to count on you all the way. If you back me today, you'll have to back me to the end of the line."

"We understand that," Bridges said. "We want you to accept."

Collier considered the offer and the board members waited, not moving. Then he walked around the long table and sat down at the head of it. They smiled and nodded as though a large responsibility had been lifted from them.

"The first thing I intend to do is to order an inquest held in the death of Jim Enright. Judge Waller can preside and set the date for it. Joe, conduct a complete, private investigation of the matter and keep it confidential. Clyde Meers will be pestering the hell out of you for a story, but don't give him anything."

"All right, Adam."

"Gentlemen, there seem to be two possibilities here. Jim was waylaid by toughs who either had previous knowledge that he was a winner, or who took a chance on him having money on him. In either case, Roan Spencer, Fred Carlyle, and Bill Frame should be strongly suspected until they are cleared satisfactorily. That goes for anyone else we may find who had knowledge of that game, and anyone who knew Enright was going home the winner."

Stiles said, "Adam, we all know these men; you're good friends with all three. Do you think we ought to—"

"When we talk about murder," Adam Collier said, "I think we're within our rights to ask for more than a man's word. We'll proceed with the inquiry. I'll talk to Judge Waller this morning about it."

"Just what do you expect to find out?" Bridges wanted to know.

"Who is innocent, as well as who is guilty," Collier said. "It's also about time we enacted some legislation to effect a few changes in Bonanza." He looked around the table. "I'm talking about a city property tax to support a police force large enough to keep the peace."

"Oh, I don't think you could get enough people behind it to pass it," Bridges said.

"You bought the fire department," Collier pointed out.

"But the county pays for it, too," Bridges said.

"This is something we're going to talk about," Collier promised. "And this afternoon at one o'clock. Try not to be late."

Jeff Stiles blew out his breath, then laughed. "Well," he said, "I told you it would go this way, didn't I?" He got up and put on his hat. "If the meeting's over, I've got a store to take care of."

They got up and left, but Joe Beal remained. After the door closed, he lit a cigar and puffed it for a moment. "I started on the police force in New York fifteen years ago. Maybe I could give you help or advice."

"I'd appreciate it. Could you work up a table of organization, something similar to what I have in the fire department?"

"Sure. You want it at one o'clock?"

"Yes. I'm going to have to sell this fast or not at all." Collier shook his head. "We've never had any law in this town. Sure, we've always had a marshal and a night deputy, but that doesn't guarantee law and order in a town this size in which any man can carry a gun if he feels like it. How many men would you say it would take to police this town?"

"Twenty," Beal said. "Four during the day and sixteen at night. But it'll take more than cops, Adam. It'll take some city ordinances with teeth in them, and I don't know as you'll get those passed."

"We'll try."

Beal shrugged. "That's all a man can do. Try."

He left, and Collier returned to the firehouse where he wrote a note to his wife, gave it to one of the firemen to deliver, then walked to the newspaper office. Clyde Meers was writing an obituary. He put his pen aside and swiveled his chair around when Collier sat down.

Meers said, "Pete Madden stopped in and told me you'd been appointed mayor. To be honest with you, Adam, I'd have preferred a more conservative man. You're a crusader, and reformers make me nervous."

"Be at the meeting at one o'clock," Collier advised.

"I wouldn't think of missing it," Meers said. "Who do you think will get the directorship of the bank? Enright had no children." He brushed his mustache. "Madden tells me you're going to have an inquest."

"He deserves that. You don't just find a man dead alongside the road and shrug it off."

"That," Meers pointed out, "seems to be the way things are in Bonanza."

"So? That makes it all right?" Collier got up. "I'd like to see your back issues, Clyde. The last four years."

Adam Collier expected some kind of a turnout at the one o'clock board meeting, but he did not expect the room to be as packed as it was. Every saloon-owner along Gold Street was present, and there were few bawdy houses and dance halls that did not have a spokesman present. The solid merchants were there, both local attorneys, and two of the town's doctors: Stover Ainsley, and a younger man.

Collier rapped for silence and got it. They were eager to hear what he had to say.

"The meeting will come to order." The mayor glanced at the clerk who had his book open and pen in hand. "Gentlemen, since I left this room earlier this morning, I've done some checking and have compiled a record of crime in our fine city. So as not to bore you, I've gone back only four years. May I read? In that time, we have had thirteen murders; Jim Enright's death brings the total to fourteen. There have been eighty-six robberies resulting in bodily injury. Seven women have been molested on Gold Street, and the only reason that there have not been more attacks is that husbands don't permit their wives to step out of their homes at night."

"So it's a rough town," one man said. "What of it?"

"I'll tell you 'what of it' in a moment," Collier

answered coolly. "To date, there have been no convictions of any person or persons for these crimes. I do not imply that Judge Waller's court has been remiss in its duty, but insufficient evidence has been the factor affecting this immunity to law." He looked at the merchants sitting solemnly silent. "How many of you have had your stores damaged by toughs? Or, perhaps, I should ask: how many of you have *not* had your property damaged? No hands? Not one solitary hand?" He pointed. "Peterson, how many times have you had merchandise ruined and your place damaged by some drunk who thought he owned the world?"

The man thought about it. "I guess seven or eight times. It's expensive."

"That's right, it's expensive. And you saloon-owners along the main street—you're constantly replacing glasses and tables and mirrors. Why, the freight company pays their overhead off the profit they make just hauling in replacement equipment for you."

Bill Frame said, "That's part of the business, Adam. We all know that and accept it."

"*You* don't."

"What do you mean? The hell I don't."

"I say that you don't," Collier said, "because you employ your own private police force on a 'round-the-clock basis. When was the last time you were really busted up?"

Frame let a smile build slowly. "I get your point. Oh, a good three years now."

"You may get it," Pete Madden said, "but I don't."

"All right, I'll explain it then," Collier said. "I want this town cleaned up. I want the toughs driven out or put in jail. I want to see it so that, when a man walks into a store, the owner doesn't have to wonder if hell's going to break loose. I want every business house in this town to start paying city taxes so that we can employ a full-time police force of sufficient strength to maintain law and order."

They all wanted to talk at once. Clyde Meers was writing furiously; this was the kind of copy that would sell newspapers. Finally, Adam Collier rapped for silence and got it.

"Mr. Clayborn, the city attorney, can advise you of your rights," the mayor continued, "but I can tell you right now that the city council has the authority to levy taxes in such amounts as they deem necessary to support a proper city government and its functions. And if we levy taxes, we will also collect them."

"You'll get mine with a gun," one man said.

Adam Collier pointed the handle of the gavel at him and sighted over it. "Friend, if I have to, I'll collect your taxes with a big stick, and I'll get the money, or the value, out of your hide. And you'd better believe it." He glanced slowly at everyone in the room. "Before you start howling about how much this is going to cost you, consider how much it costs you right now to maintain your places of business and you'll find that taxes used to protect you are a bargain."

"Police won't stop a man from wrecking a store," one merchant insisted.

"Perhaps, at first, they won't," Collier said, "but it will put a few toughs in jail and the court can make *them* pay for the damages. In time, when we convince the hoodlums that this town is a real unhealthy place for them to live in, you won't have to worry about breakage."

"We already pay county taxes and get damned little for it," Bill Frame objected. "Adam, I don't think this is right."

Frame heard a chorus of approving voices behind him; Collier let the talk go on for a moment, then he brought the meeting back to order.

"Mr. Clayborn has the tax structure the county uses as a base for assessment, and I've asked him to adapt a scale for city use. Would you give us your recommendations?" Collier asked the lawyer.

"Certainly," Clayborn said. He was a thin, taciturn man, sick of his emasculated role as city attorney. "The legitimate businesshouses which keep books, and all of them do, will be taxed on a two per cent gross rate, and pay a fifty-dollar-a-year business license fee."

There was a moment of sighing, of apparent relief among the businessmen; a few of them looked at each other and smiled for they were getting off easier than they had expected.

Clayborn continued: "Gambling halls, saloons, dance halls, and houses of prostitution are, by and large, to be considered 'places of amusement' and, as such, do not keep books. In lieu of a tax, a fee for a business license for such an operation should be established amounting to fifteen hundred dollars per year."

One man sprang to his feet. "What kind of a skin game is this?" he roared. " 'Places of amusement?' "

Collier eyed him coldly. "Arents, are you going to tell me that a whorehouse is a necessity?"

"Christ, there must be at least forty in town!"

Collier rapped with his gavel. "I'm not going to sit here all day and listen to you people jabber! You

clean the pockets of the miners every payday, oper-
ate on as low an overhead as possible, and bitch
because your three-hundred per cent profit isn't
enough." He glanced at the board members. "Gentlemen, the chair will entertain a motion to adopt a
city tax rate."

Pete Madden said, "I so move."

Howard Bridges, who never said much anyway,
rose to second the motion. Collier called for a vote
amid the uproar which followed and the measure
was passed.

Turning to Joe Beal, Collier said, "Will you please
clear the room of everyone except Judge Waller, Mr.
Clayborn, and Clyde Meers. The merchants can stay
if they remain orderly." He smiled. "I don't see
many of them making a fuss anyway."

Threats were flung at Collier and the town council
so fast and so loud that the sounds of them inter-
mingled and none of them were quite clear. Beal
had to get a little rough with several men, but he
cleared the room and locked the door. Collier sighed
and lit a cigar.

Meers said, "I have to give you credit, Adam,
you're a hell of a lot better politician than I realized."

"Frankly," Madden admitted, "I was against the
city tax, dead set against it." He smiled, and added,
"But, it was such a good deal, I just couldn't pass it
up. The places of—ah—amusement are going to
carry the biggest share of the load."

"Why not?" Clayborn asked stiffly. "They make
the most profit. Besides, who needs those dens anyway?" A wan smile played on his lips. "When Adam
approached me, I really didn't think there was much

hope. Enright had discussed this problem with me from time to time. But I could see Adam's point: get the merchants behind it and it would pass. First, we must protect the solid elements in our town."

"What a story!" Meers said. "But, of course, you haven't collected any taxes yet, and that may be another story. An even better one!"

Chapter Eight

Three weeks went by before the paper work was finished and the notices and statements went out. They were delivered by three men Judge Waller deputized for the purpose. Since this was not a pleasant job, several times the deputies were called on to protect themselves from angry owners of back-street houses.

There was a thirty-day grace period in which to pay the taxes, and all the solid merchants along Gold Street paid without protest. They filed estimates based on the previous six-month's gross and brought their money to the courthouse to be deposited in the safe there.

Judge Waller, unhappy with the job, issued ninety-one writs of attachment on various "places of amusement." Then he went to bed with a severe headache and a premonition of disaster. Joe Beal, backed by eight deputies, all armed with ax handles and pistols, set out to collect the taxes or close the places permanently.

Beal's first stop was a saloon on Gold Street and trouble waited for him just inside the door—a line of bouncers. In an efficient, legal manner, Beal announced his intentions; then the bouncers went into action.

Beal and his men were occupied for almost an

hour in their collections. Two deputies were knocked unconscious and required a bit of sewing in the scalp area, but, the next morning, when Judge Waller held court, he had seventeen defendants before the bench and the total fines meted out came to a little over seven thousand dollars. During his rest, Waller had remembered where he had misplaced that heavy book, and, once he had found it, he threw it at the guilty.

Beal and his deputies, in the process of carrying out their duties, had reduced the saloon to such a shambles that opening it without extensive repairs was out of the question. The owners took the cash they had on hand, walked away from it all, and caught the next stage out of town.

Immediately, over sixty saloons, houses of prostitution, dance halls, and gambling cribs produced the money to pay their taxes rather than risking the energetic collection methods of Joe Beal and deputies.

A few places held out, got tough about it, and Beal and his men called. Again, there was an exciting account of the fracas on the front page of Clyde Meers' newspaper. Judge Waller was beginning to find court interesting and the fines were as heavy as he thought the traffic would bear. The rest of the city taxes were soon paid and business licenses were issued.

Adam Collier, in spite of other things on his mind, did not slight his duties at the fire department although he found it impossible to spend a full day there as he had done before.

The council authorized the police force, appropriated the money for it, but this was kept out of the paper. Joe Beal interviewed and recruited men for the jobs, and once hired, they were moved to a ranch seven miles from town for training. Collier had some definite ideas about what the police force should be and he found Joe Beal pretty much in agreement. They felt that police authority should be respected rather than the man in uniform, since laws should not be enforced only because they were backed by a very fast six-shooter.

Joe Beal was spending a good deal of his time away from town which drew some critical attention, but Madden and Bridges and the other council members pretended they didn't know anything about his absences. There was some grumbling about the taxes; the money was just sitting there in the safe and not being used; the peace was being kept by two deputies while Joe Beal went chasing around to suit himself.

Friends of Jim Enright were complaining that the hearing that had been promised had never taken place and Adam Collier's name kept coming up when criticisms were made. He did not answer these attacks and Bonanza was as wild and free-wheeling a town as ever. Now and then, Adam would drop in at the Jackpot and talk to Bill Frame; twice, he sat in on a private poker game with Frame, Fred Carlyle and Roan Spencer, but, when the talk came around to reforms, Collier shrugged it off. It wouldn't, he knew, be long before the rumor of graft was circulated.

Six crates of freight arrived and were taken to the out-of-town ranch. Collier went with the wagon, telling his wife that he might be gone overnight. Joe Beal was at the ranch and they both carried the crates into the house, which had been converted into a barracks. There they uncrated the uniforms and passed them out.

The next morning, Collier had breakfast at the crack of dawn, and, by the time, it was full daylight, he went to the barn with Beal and Bonanza's police force to begin the final morning training period.

The barn had been gutted and turned into a large gymnasium. Beal explained the punching bags and various devices they had built.

"In New York, we had places like this and a cop worked out once a week. You learned to handle that night stick as well as to box and wrestle." He put his fingers in his mouth and whistled. "All right, let's get some practice with the sticks!"

The night sticks were racked along one wall, solid ash, two-and-a-half inches around, with lead-loaded handles; and each could be dangled from the wrist by a wide leather thong which hung quite loosely.

While Collier watched, two lines of men, twelve in each line, demonstrated their dexterity with the sticks.

Joe Beal asked, "Did you ever wonder why a cop keeps twirling his stick? I used to. It's practice. It keeps him familiar with it, and believe me, in the hands of a trained man, it's a damned deadly weapon. Let me show you a few things. Hey, Malloy!"

The man stepped out of ranks and grinned at Collier.

A cloth bag containing an egg was hung at fore-head height on a suspended dummy and Malloy took his position a good seven feet in front of it.

"Let's assume," Beal said, "that we have an armed man, weapon drawn and pointed at Malloy. His duty is to arrest and disarm the man." He reached into his back pocket and took out a small-caliber cap-and-ball revolver and handed it to Collier. "This contains only a wax ball, barely enough to cover the powder; we use it for a blank gun. Cock it, and when Malloy moves, you fire it into the ground, much the same as the armed man would if the officer moved. We'll see who gets who first."

"Some game," Collier said as he pointed the gun down. He jerked the trigger when Malloy flipped his arm straight out; the night stick went out like a projectile, the round end of it barely cracking the shell of the egg. "I'd have had my head broken," Collier said and handed the gun back to Beal.

"Show him what that stick can do," Beal invited and Malloy fractured one-inch boards with the end of it, used it for a lever to throw a man down, and handcuffed him with the thong.

Beal and Collier walked back toward the house while the drill went on.

"Twelve hours a day; that's the pace we've been going," Beal said, "and every man is an expert with the stick."

They stepped inside and opened a small crate of .32 Smith & Wesson pocket revolvers. Beal commented: "This, to a policeman, is a device to protect his life when all else fails. None of my men are going to shoot it out with anyone unless they're cornered. They're ready to turn loose, Adam."

"Yes, I can see that. All right, this Saturday. I'll tell Meers to announce in the paper that the fireman's band will lead a parade. We'll march the men down Gold Street and let the citizens have a good look.

They may not take what they see too seriously," Collier continued. He smiled. "Joe Beal, gunfighter. This is quite a change for you, isn't it?"

Beal shrugged his shoulders. "A man is what he has to be; I wouldn't have got very far alone with a night stick. So I kept the peace on their terms. But I never liked it. I never believed it was the best way. Hell, any New York cop with his night stick could spank the ass off any of these gunmen. The only way to get a good cop is to stand off and shoot him, and then you'd better run damned far and fast because the rest will be after you."

"I can see why you once asked me if you could make a police force out of my firemen." He offered his hand. "I'll see you Saturday, and the Bonanza Silver Cornet Fireman's Band will have their buttons polished."

He went outside and found Malloy waiting for him. "I could fight you now, Mayor."

Collier shook his head and laughed. "After what I've seen, I wouldn't touch you with a ten-foot pole." He looked at Malloy. "A cop. By golly, I didn't know. Is it what you want?"

"Yes," Malloy said. "I'll be a good cop, Mayor."

"I know that." Adam untied his horse, mounted, and rode back to town.

It was afternoon when he reached Clyde Meers' office and found the man red-eyed and uncertainly postured in his swivel chair. "My boy," Meers said, "you are looking at a man destroyed by the prosaic doings of a dull, spiritless town. Join me in a drink. I shall drink to forget my misery and you will drink to forget you saw me drunk."

"I've got something for your paper."

"Indeed? A proclamation perhaps? The world can always stand a good proclamation; it gives a man something to forget."

"We're going to have a little parade Saturday at noon to introduce the new police force to Bonanza."

"Indeed," Meers said, pushing his bottle aside. "Adam, you interest me no end. The details, if you don't mind. I promise you this will get plenty of space on the front page."

Joe Beal brought his police officers into town in plain, run-of-the-mill street dress which attracted no attention at all. They put their uniforms on at the fire station—blue uniforms with double rows of bright brass buttons and shell hats with emblems dominating their crowns. Badges had been shined and shoes had been highly polished; the night sticks had been carefully sanded and varnished. Drawn up in their exact formation, they were, Collier thought, capable of passing the most demanding military inspection. The men were all tall; their mustaches were properly trimmed; their leather chin straps were hooked precisely on the point of the chin.

Beal's uniform was the same as the officers' except he wore a blue kepi and his badge, buttons, and emblem were silver. The firemen, long regimented to order and duty, were impressed, but Collier knew that the toughs along Gold Street wouldn't be. He took Beal to one side and cautioned, "Feel free to halt the parade at any time, for any reason you see fit."

"I'll do just that if I have to," Beal said. "We're ready if you are."

The ten-piece band was tuned and ready to march

and the bass drummer began his beat; with the cornets leading, the police force left the fire station, quick stepping to "Dixie."

Collier worked his way through the crowd jamming Gold Street, took a side route, and got on the porch of the Jackpot so he would have a good view. All traffic had been halted. He turned his head when he heard Roan Spencer speak.

"There's nothing like a parade, Adam. What's the occasion? New uniforms for the firemen?"

Bill Frame took his cigar from his mouth. "Look again. They're policemen."

The crowd was becoming aware of this and, as the parade traveled down the street, the men lining the walk wondered what to make of it. They were a fine sight, twenty-four men, night sticks swinging in unison, eyes to the front, marching to the band. Collier let his glance leave them and travel ahead, looking for the trouble. He found it—a knot of six men who moved out into the street, not into the path of the marchers, but nearer to them than the rest of the crowd. As they approached, the hecklers began to hoot and call out.

"Little boy blue, come blow my horn!"

"Hell, they ain't even carryin' guns!"

"Oh, ain't that sweet now?"

Joe Beal held up his hand and the parade stopped. He did a precise about face and snapped: "Officer Malloy, will you quiet that disturbance, please?"

"Did you hear that? He said 'please'! Ain't that sweet?"

Malloy saluted and left the ranks; he marched up to the rowdies smartly and said: "Move along now before I run you in for disturbing the peace."

"Run who in?" one said; then he made the mistake of his life—he swung at Malloy's head.

Quickly, he was thrown to the ground, then Malloy seemed to be the center of a violent swirl; his night stick flashed in the sunlight and men dropped as though they were suddenly exhausted. In fifteen seconds, Malloy had finished his display and the six men were sitting on the ground, moaning, or else stretched out completely and not moving at all.

Someone shouted, "Keerist! They didn't even knock his damned hat off!"

The street was so silent that Joe Beal's words were heard clearly. "Officer Malloy, you are excused from the parade. Command what assistance you feel is necessary from the crowd and take the prisoners to jail."

"Yes, sir!"

Joe Beal spoke and turned slowly in a complete circle. "I have twenty-four men in my force. Would another half dozen care to step out and try their luck? No? It didn't seem to me that they would. I want you to remember something: Bonanza is not a good town to get tough in. There will not be a time, day or night, when a citizen is so far away from one of these officers that a call for help will not bring a policeman on the run. We're posting a warning now: behave yourself, or get out." He glanced at the bandmaster. "Let's get on with the parade."

The band began to play and the police force marched on. One of the spectators standing near the hotel said, "I wonder how good they'll be in stopping a bullet?"

Roan Spencer looked at him and replied, "It would be kind of stupid to find out, wouldn't it?"

He put his cigar in his mouth and puffed on it. "I've never seen the like of it, Adam. I recognize some local boys there. Where have you kept 'em hidden anyway?"

"We had a ranch out of town. Trained there. They're what Bonanza has needed for a long time."

"They'll take some getting used to all right," Spencer admitted. He thumped Bill Frame on the shoulder. "Looks like some law's finally come to town, boy."

"Yeah, it looks like," Frame said. His glance touched Adam Collier. "You could have taken me into your confidence, Adam. By golly, sometimes I don't think you have any thought for a friend's feelings at all." He turned and pushed back into his place. Spencer and Collier looked after him until he disappeared.

"Now that was a funny thing to say," Spencer opined.

"Bill's not easy to understand sometimes. Care for a drink?"

"Aw, the place is too crowded."

"Let's go over and nip from Meers' bottle."

Spencer thought about it. "I can't stand the windbag, but his liquor is inviting. Let's go."

Chapter Nine

The special deputies who had assisted Joe Beal in his duties as tax collector were hired on a permanent basis, a move that Collier admitted was both practical and political. Two of them were appointed as civil deputies and court bailiff, and the other four were hired as jailers as many of Bonanza's rougher citizens were taking up long residencies there.

Judge Waller began the inquiry into Jim Enright's death on a Monday morning in his court on the first floor of the county building. The subpoenas, which had been served the previous Friday, took a few people by surprise.

Since the inquest was not a trial, the courtroom was cleared; there were no jurymen sitting in the box; witnesses waited in an adjoining room, and the bailiff summoned them one at a time.

Roan Spencer was first. He was sworn in and took his place in the witness chair. Adam Collier and Joe Beal sat at the defense attorney's table; the clerk had a separate desk, and Phillip Clayborn asked the questions for the court.

"Mr. Spencer, this poker game, was it planned ahead of time or did it just happen?"

"We had a general agreement. One week at one place and the next week some place else."

"You had a schedule?"

"No, before we broke up each week we decided where we'd meet next."

"Who arrived first on the night in question?"

"Bill Frame. Enright came next, then Carlyle."

"I see," Clayborn said, casually putting his hands in his pockets. "Did you usually play for very high stakes as you did that night?"

"No. Now and then, we did, when someone felt real lucky. If one of us wanted to push the game, we did. But, generally, none of us would win or lose more than a few hundred dollars."

"Just a friendly game?"

"That's right—just a friendly game."

"Tell me," Clayborn asked, "were you interrupted at any time during the game? By that, I mean: did anyone enter your office who wasn't there to play poker?"

"No one did, no."

"But there were men at the mine?"

"Yes," Spencer said.

"Anyone who happened by could have seen Enright's buggy parked by the building entrance?"

"I suppose they could have. We weren't trying to hide anything."

"Of course not. What kind of a conveyence did Bill Frame have?"

"He rode a horse," Spencer said. "He always does."

"And Carlyle?"

"A buggy. His wife has some fancy ideas you know. My rig was in the stable behind the building. Enright rode poorly and always drove a buggy." The witness crossed his legs and folded his hands and waited for the next question.

"Who left the room while the game was in progress?"

"No one to my knowledge. Bill Frame was the first to leave. I thought at the time that he was tired and wanted to get back and check the receipts and go to bed. The game broke up shortly after that."

"When was the last time you saw Jim Enright alive?"

"Just before he closed the door to my office," Spencer said. "He waved and said good night. I never saw Jim alive again."

"I think that will be all, Mr. Spencer."

"You may step down," Judge Waller said. "Bailiff, call Fred Carlyle."

Carlyle came in as Spencer went out. He was sworn in, and Clayborn went through basically the same procedure. Carlyle had been the last to leave the game because he had stayed on an hour talking mining with Spencer. Materially, he had nothing to add except that, by remaining with Spencer, he proved that he could not have killed Enright—an hour with a good team was enough time to take any man from the mine to town, and Enright was dead before Carlyle and Spencer said good night.

After excusing Carlyle, Judge Waller asked the bailiff to bring Bill Frame in. The bar-owner was sworn in. He folded his hands and waited. Phillip Clayborn walked up and down a bit, then asked, "Mr. Frame, will you describe the night that Jim Enright died."

"I'm not sure I understand what you mean."

"I mean—was it a clear night? Cloudy? Was there a moon? Stars? What *kind* of a night was it?"

Frame gnawed his lip a moment. "Clear, I'd say."

"Is that all?"

He shrugged. "What more do you want?"

"Mr. Frame, you're a trained army officer with considerable experience. Please recall the details of the weather and atmosphere that night for the court."

"Well, the moon had gone down by the time I left town, but the sky was clear and several stars were out. Visibility was good. That is to say, one had no difficulty seeing the road clearly, or anyone on it."

"On your return to town did you see anyone?"

"Not a soul," Frame said. "The ore wagons had stopped running hours before; there was no one on the road, or in sight."

"How can you be sure the ore wagons had stopped?"

"The dust had settled completely. Generally, it hangs in the air and there is a strong oppressiveness from it for at least an hour. But there was no dust in the air, so I must conclude that the wagons had stopped running a good time before I passed through."

"And did you stop anywhere between Spencer's mine and town?"

"No," Frame said. "I simply rode straight to town."

"You saw no sign of Enright's buggy behind you?"

"No, because I never looked behind. I left first and have no exact idea when he left." He unfolded his hands and placed them on his knees. "Are you trying to establish that I killed Jim Enright, counselor?"

Judge Waller said, "The time of your arrival in

town has been substantiated by police investigation, and I rather think our purpose now is to establish your alibi for the time Enright was killed. To have killed him would have necessitated your waiting for him, and, of course, we have to consider carefully the element of time. Do you have any further questions, Mr. Clayborn?"

"Yes, your honor." The attorney addressed the witness. "Are there witnesses as to the time you arrived in Bonanza?"

Frame considered for a moment. "I ran into Doc Stover and Clyde Meers and had a drink with them. They could establish the time."

"Then you may step down. I will now call Joseph Beal."

Joe Beal took the stand and answered the preliminary questions put to him. He said, "Although Bill Frame didn't mention this, there wasn't much of a wind that night, and, by the early morning hours, it had died down completely. Since there was little traffic on the road, I was able to put together a pretty good picture by the tracks we found. You see, Enright was found by the first ore wagon that came through the next day, and his body was brought to town immediately. I went to the place the attack occurred and looked around very carefully. Frame's horse left distinct tracks; he did not stop at any time. As you know, a horse will stamp around when halted; there were no tracks to indicate this. There were, however, signs that two men had been hiding among the rocks—for how long, I couldn't say since neither left any signs other than a few tracks. They evidently saw the buggy and jumped it as it started to pass then; it was halted immediately."

"Were these men mounted then?" Clayborn asked.

"No, they were afoot. Enright was evidently struck; then he fell out of the buggy. There was blood on the seat, but the largest share of it was on the ground. Apparently, several blows were struck after he fell on the ground. Then one man left and brought up the horses and the killers mounted and rode toward town. Of course, their tracks were lost completely the moment they reached Gold Street."

"You found no other traces of them then?"

"No, sir, although I can give you a pretty accurate description of the men. One was taller than the other; I'd say nearly six-feet. The second man was considerably shorter; he was the one who actually killed Jim Enright. His tracks were profuse around the buggy; the tall man with the lengthy stride got the horses. Occupationally, the evidence suggests that both men are not miners; their boots had high, riding heels; they are probably cattlemen and, possibly, work around here on one of the ranches."

"Well, that's quite a lot to go on," Clayborn admitted.

"I'm not quite finished," Beal said. "The short man is left-handed; this is apparent from the position of the blow which he struck Enright. At first, I thought this was merely a necessity since he mounted the off side, but the blows struck on the ground were also laid on with the left hand."

"I hardly find that conclusive," Judge Waller said.

Beal looked at him. "Yes, I wondered about it too, but at the farm, where the police were trained, I experimented a bit. I would put a stick in the left hand of a right-handed man, have him beat a grain bag, and invariably he would strike the first blow with his off hand, find it clumsy, and switch the stick to his other hand. Eight men did this in a row without knowing what I was looking for. So I am convinced that we are looking for a rather short, left-handed man who chews tobacco." He smiled when Clayborn raised his eyebrows. "Yes, sir, he *chews* smoking tobacco. Plug has sweeteners in it and, even when dried, it has a peculiar odor. Smoking tobacco does not, and the samples I found in the dust indicate that he chews pipe tobacco."

"That certainly is odd," Clayborn said. "Pipe tobacco is rather bitter when chewed."

"If a man had false teeth," Beal said, "then it wouldn't be so odd, would it? Cut plug is rather tough to chew with false teeth."

"By God, now, it wouldn't!" Clayborn said quickly. He smiled and his eyes took on a brilliance. "I trust, Mr. Beal, that you enjoy keeping the court in suspense. Did you learn any more?"

"It's my opinion that Enright was deliberately murdered, either because he recognized his assailant, or that the man who killed him just wanted to kill someone. Certainly, the first blow struck must have been fatal or nearly so; Dr. Stover says the skull was fractured in three places, indicating a solid object swung with considerable force. So we are assured that Enright never fought back." He scratched his mustache a moment. "We're dealing in theory now, not physical evidence, so I'd like to advance a bit further, with your permission, your honor."

"I see no reason why you should not," Waller said.

Beal related his experience with the man in the cage; he left nothing out of the proposition that had been made to him. "So I believe," he went on, "that

Enright's killing was motivated by robbery and it was carried out by an organized gang of cutthroats. Despite the large sum we know was taken, the killers probably received only a small share, or a set fee for doing the job. The rest went into the pocket of the man who controls crime in Bonanza."

"It's likely that you're right," Judge Waller said, "but it must be obvious to this man that you don't intend to keep the bargain and he'll mark you for killing."

"A decoy may be what we need," Beal said, "and if we're lucky, we may catch two fish, one short, one tall, and one of them left-handed with false teeth."

"I have no further questions, your honor," Clayborn said.

"Then the witness may step down. I think it's time for some lunch and a drink. This inquiry will resume at two o'clock. I caution you to maintain silence on what has gone on here." Judge Waller rapped his gavel and the men got up and stirred restlessly.

Beal left the stand and walked over to Adam Collier.

"I think you're taking a damned foolish chance," Collier told him. "Somehow this will leak out—what's been said here today."

"That's all right," Beal said. "I'm ready to spring my own trap." He looked around to see if everyone had left the room. "Remember that friend I had in San Francisco? He's here. Got in last night. Tonight, he's going to be a big winner." He reached for pencil and paper on the defense table and drew a rough sketch. "This is the alley behind the Jackpot; that's where I'll be, ready to change places with him. We've already worked out the details on what we'll be wearing. There's a bunch of wooden crates about thirty yards south of the Jackpot, just after you enter the alley. We'll make the switch there." He made a mark on the paper. "You be waiting here, in this doorway; it's a hide house the harness maker uses and the door will be open. I suggest you use a shotgun." He balled the paper and put it in his pocket. "If I'm not waylaid in that alley, I'll miss my guess. But if I'm not, stay behind me far enough to give the toughs a chance at me."

"If there's any mistake, any slip———"

"There's always that chance, but it's better than not being prepared." Beal smiled and brushed his sweeping mustache. "Adam, I've been working on a sawed-off shotgun, something special for this. I got hold of a small-bore bird gun, a 16 gauge, sawed it off to eight inches, and embedded some lead in the chopped stock. I'm going to use slugs; I want to stop these men but I don't want to kill them. Of course, if I fail to stop them, you'll have to kill them, so use double-O buckshot."

Collier nodded. "Joe, I hope you understand this, but I'm a great believer in the due process of law. It would be a lot better all the way around if you put a few police in the alley———"

"They'll be watching for that," Beal said. "Adam, don't let me down now."

"Hell, I wouldn't do that. What time?"

"Midnight," Beal said and went out.

Collier had been spending so much time away from his home and family that he felt a twinge of conscience about it so, before supper, he weeded the garden, put new leathers in the pump, and cleaned out the shed where junk always seemed to accumulate.

After supper, he helped June wash the dishes, without breaking any of them, then read to the children until it was their bedtime. By eight-thirty, the house was quiet, Collier was enjoying his cigar and his newspaper, and June was busy with her mending.

She said, "You certainly have been ambitious this evening, your honor. Do you mind if it makes me a little suspicious?"

"How could you think a thing like that?" he asked, smiling behind his paper.

June got up, went over and sat on his lap, putting his paper on the floor and his cigar in a glass dish.

"I've always been sure that you were meant to be an important man, Adam. I don't think you could do anything that wasn't done well. But think of us. Think of where we would be if anything happened to you."

"The funny thing of it is," he said, that I'm not really very brave. I never have been. During the war and many times before and after, I've had to stiffen myself to meet the trouble that came my way. I've always envied Bill Frame because he could take chances that would make your hair stand on end and get away with it. Me, I never could do that. Do you understand what I'm telling you? I'll do what I believe I must do because I'm that way, but I would not take a risk just to be taking it."

"Are you going out tonight?"

"Very late," he said. "Around midnight." He looked at her. "What made you ask?"

"Because I saw you take your shotgun out of the shed and put it in the hall closet." June kissed him and patted his cheek before getting off his lap. "There ought to be a lot of other places to live, Adam, places that are safer than Bonanza."

"Do you want to go somewhere else?"

She smiled and shook her head. "I'm like you, Adam; I wouldn't want to miss out on anything either. I never could break myself from peeking into cooking pots and rattling packages before I opened them. I'll be awake when you get back."

"Get your sleep," he said, but he knew that she meant what she said.

Chapter Ten

His name was O'Hagen and he wore a good suit and a diamond stickpin and his gambling game cards; he could play them any way a man wanted them played—straight or crooked. O'Hagen was in his late twenties, a handsome man with a fawn mustache, very pale eyes, and no visible scars on his face, which meant that he could duck extremely well or had never been caught dealing from the bottom of the deck.

He went into the Jackpot, had a whiskey and some cold cuts at the free-lunch counter, then bought into a small game. O'Hagen had not played thirty minutes before he ran the table stakes up so high that new blood was needed.

Chairs were vacated and filled with men with fatter pokes, and, by ten o'clock, a good crowd had formed around his table and O'Hagen's winnings were impressive enough to make any man's eyes a little rounder.

Jake Powell came in, saw what was going on, and went in back to Bill Frame's office. He didn't use the hall door, but went on down and stepped into the liquor storeroom, carefully closing the door. He made his way across the cluttered room without falling or touching anything and uncovered a peephole in the wall. Frame was alone in his office, so Jake rapped lightly twice and pushed open a small door.

A section of France's bookcase opened and Jake bent his head and entered. He closed the hidden door and said, "There's a fancy-dresser out there who's winning big, Bill."

"How much?"

"At least five or six thousand right now."

Frame brushed a hand across his smooth cheek. "That's a lot of money for one man to have. What kind of a game is he playing?"

"Fast. Looks straight to me though."

"A man riding his luck, huh?" Frame waved his hand. "Go on back and watch awhile. I'll be out." He watched Jake Powell step to the hidden door, then said, "After I come out, get BooBoo and hang around. You never can tell."

"Sure," Powell said and left.

Bill Frame waited fifteen minutes, then left his office by the hall door and went into the big room; he had no trouble spotting the big game. He gently elbowed his way in so that he was standing next to the table. He watched the play, watched O'Hagen handle the cards; the man was obviously a professional, but Frame could not detect anything wrong with his shuffle or deal.

When one of the men threw in and backed out of the game, Frame sat down and smiled. "My name's Frame; I own the place. You don't mind, Mr——"

"O'Hagen. No, money's money. Five-card stud?"

"One poison is as good as another," Frame commented, and the game began.

Frame knew how to keep a lot of money on the

table, yet not lose or win much himself. He talked a lot and checked his hand a lot when he felt the cards were not going right. Other men came and went in the game and, finally, at eleven-thirty, O'Hagen pushed back his chair and got up. "I thank you for a pleasant evening, gentlemen."

As O'Hagen gathered his loaded pokes, Bill Frame spoke around his cigar. "My cashier will change that into something less bulky, friend."

"It might be easier to handle at that," O'Hagen said and followed Frame over to the cashier's wicket. A shotgun guard stood nearby and he eyed O'Hagen suspiciously while he waited for his winnings to be counted. They came to nearly fourteen thousand dollars; O'Hagen requested gold because he was going back to San Francisco and paper money wasn't very popular there.

When the gold had been tucked away in O'Hagen's belt, Frame said, "It's a policy of my establishment to escort winners to their lodging. There are toughs about, you know, and——"

"——in San Francisco, we have the Sidney Ducks," O'Hagen said. "I'll manage by myself, thanks."

"A man walking shotgun——"

"He'd make me nervous. Thanks just the same." O'Hagen smiled, elbowed his way out of the bar, and paused on the front porch a moment, looking up and down the street. He did not see Joe Beal at first, but when he stepped off the porch and walked along, he saw the marshal, dressed in an old coat and hat, leave a crack between two buildings. Beal walked along the other side, staying abreast of O'Hagen.

Farther down, on the same side as O'Hagen, Adam Collier moved along, half-hidden by the throngs of men milling on the narrow walk. When he saw O'Hagen turn the corner, Collier worked his way to the alley by the first convenient gap between buildings; he came out behind a clothing store and saw O'Hagen standing far down near the alley's mouth.

Collier waited, wondering what O'Hagen was standing there for, then O'Hagen turned and disappeared down the alley. Collier arrived across from the alley and stopped; he didn't have to wait long before Jake and BooBoo Powell came along.

Jake said something and jerked his head to point down the alley into which O'Hagen had disappeared. Across the street, a man clad in an old coat and hat lounged against a dark wall. Collier's view was limited to an empty portion of the street and the alley maw across, but he heard a man shout: "Joe! Joe Beal! Wait up there!"

Then Clyde Meers hurried into view, cutting over to where Beal lounged against the wall. Without hesitation, Jake and BooBoo Powell hurried on, now warned that they had almost stepped into something dangerous.

The entire plan was over, finished, blown skyhigh, so Collier left the alley and walked over to Joe Beal who was trying to contain his fury.

"Now what the hell did I do?" Meers asked pleadingly. "Hell, I saw you, and wondered what the devil you were doing in that getup. Anything wrong with that?"

Collier took a cigar from his pocket and handed it to Beal. "Take a couple of puffs on this before you answer."

He turned as O'Hagen came from the alley and approached them.

He looked curiously at Meers and asked, "Who the hell is he?"

"Who the hell are *you* to be asking who the hell *I* am?" Meers snapped. He turned his head and glared at Joe Beal. "What's goin' on here? Adam?"

"Police business," Beal said. "That's all I can say, Clyde. And if I told you more, it wouldn't be for publication anyway."

"Well, it looks funny to me," Meers said and walked back toward the main street.

"I'd like to——"

"Cool off, Joe," O'Hagen said. "He didn't know." He turned his head to look in the direction the Powell brothers had taken. "They smelled a rat right away, didn't they?"

"You'd better get out of town," Beal said. "Within an hour, every tough in Bonanza will know what you look like and will be after you. Besides, you've done all you could here, Sean. Spend your winnings wisely in San Francisco."

"It was a tidy profit all right," O'Hagen admitted. "It makes me feel guilty, trimmin' the suckers that way and——"

"Sooner or later, it would have gone into the tough's pockets anyway," Collier said. "Goodbye, Mr. O'Hagen, and thanks for trying."

"Now, now, don't be pushin' a man off so quick like that," he said. "Sure now, I ought to be of some use. I did ride all the way from San Francisco, did I not? It seems to me that all that money I'll be carrying around town will be an attraction to the toughs and they may try again."

"They know by now that we used you for bait," Beal said. "Why take chances?"

"It's part of my business, Joe. You wouldn't run me out now, would you?"

"No."

"Then I'll take up quarters in the hotel and live in a grand manner, something befittin' a big winner's style."

"The toughs will have you marked," Collier warned.

"Aye, and I'll have them marked." He looked at Joe Beal's sawed-off shotgun. "Now that's a handy little thing for close work, isn't it? You wouldn't loan that to a friend, would you?"

Beal gave him the gun and some spare shells; O'Hagen put it under his coat. He touched his fingers to his hat, smiled, and went toward the main street and the hotel.

"That's quite a friend," Collier said. "I hope he sleeps light."

"He does," Beal said.

They went their separate ways. Collier went into his house quietly, trying not to wake his wife, but she was awake and lighted the lamp as he put the shotgun against a chair and took off his clothes.

"Didn't it come off, Adam?"

"No," he said, and pulled on his nightshirt.

"Before Sissy went to bed, she told me you said she could have a dog."

He looked at her, puzzled, then snapped his finger. "She did ask me, nearly a month ago. I said I'd think about it." He shook his head and blew out the lamp. "Don't kids ever forget?"

"Not what they want to remember," she said and moved against him.

* * *

Sean O'Hagen took a room at the hotel, bought a newspaper at the desk, and whistled while walking up to the second floor. When he put the key in the lock, he noticed that it was hardly a key at all, just a bent piece of metal with a shallow groove in it; the door could be opened with a bent wire as easily as with the key.

He was still whistling as he stepped inside and lit the lamp. He drew the shades and put the paper on the bed; then he took a jackknife from his pocket and sliced a heavy sliver a foot long from the pine door frame. He opened the door, wedged this sliver in between door and frame near the top hinge, then forced it closed; he tested the sliver and figured it would hold at last two pounds without bending or breaking. Then he locked the door from the inside. He went to the bed and patiently untied some of the yarn ties of the quilt. Knotting these together, he tied one end to the handle of the empty water pitcher and the other to the sliver so that the pitcher was precariously suspended nearly six feet from the floor.

Then he stretched out on the bed, read the paper, and, finally, undressed and went to bed, falling immediately into a sound sleep, the sawed-off shotgun lying beside him on the bed.

The crash of the pitcher woke O'Hagen and he saw the outline of the door opening; he fired and the heavy slug went through the door, through the intruder's chest, and slapped into the wall across the hall. There was a drumming of feet on the stairs, a man running down, but this did not concern O'Hagen at all. He pulled his pants on casually, lit the lamp, then refreshed the spent chamber of the shotgun.

The shot had aroused everyone on the floor and the night clerk came booming up the stairs, yelling to be let through. He saw the dead man, let out a frightened bleat, and began yelling for the law.

Officer Malloy and another policeman arrived. Malloy did the questioning while his partner cleared the hall and made everyone go back to their rooms.

"I'll start with your name," Malloy said to the Irishman. He proceeded to write everything down that was said.

O'Hagen volunteered answers without hesitation. Then Malloy inspected the broken pitcher and the fallen sliver.

"That's very clever," he said. "Did you think of that?"

"I did," O'Hagen admitted. "A man has to learn to take care of himself, Officer. Many places he frequents might have no locks on the doors at all. Something loud and sudden always brings me awake."

"Then you were expectin' company?" Malloy asked.

"Yes. I think we ought to talk to Joe Beal about this."

"That we will," Malloy said.

They stepped out into the hall. There was a blanket over the dead man.

Malloy said, "I sent the clerk for some help and a stretcher. We'll take the body over to the chief's office and try and identify it before we cart it to the undertaker." He looked at Sean O'Hagen. "Ain't you the big winner from Frame's place?"

"Big enough to attract trouble," O'Hagen said.

Although it was a quarter after three, Malloy woke Joe Beal and he came out of his quarters, which were next to his office and jail. He wore his trousers with the suspenders hanging down and his hair was rumpled.

When he saw O'Hagen, Beal asked, "They didn't wait long, did they, Sean?"

"I didn't think they would."

"Malloy, you and Harding go back to your beat. You can give me a report of this in the morning."

Malloy touched his cap with his fingers and went out. The dead man was brought in and placed on a cell cot. Then the two policemen left.

Joe Beal examined the man's hat; it had matches stuck in the band. He laid it aside and went through the shirt pockets. There was a piece of Burley twist tobacco, a short letter so blood-smeared that he couldn't read it, and a pay slip from Roan Spencer's mine. Continued search turned up a twelve-inch lead truncheon, a five-shot pepperbox pocket pistol, and nine dollars in silver coins.

"Maybe we can trace him through Roan's payroll records," Beal said as he went back into his office. He slumped in his swivel chair and motioned for O'Hagen to sit down. "It always seems to end like this, a blind alley, a dead man that we can identify, maybe, but then the trail just fizzles out. You know, that can get mighty frustratin'."

"You mean the toughs knock a man on the head, rob him, and turn the money over to someone else?"

"That's right. They're on salary, and I pity the poor bastard who tries to play any other game."

O'Hagen laughed softly. "That makes the Sidney Ducks a bit amateurish. They work only in small gangs." He leaned forward and helped himself to one of Beal's cigars. "You've got a game goin' here that sounds interestin' to a man of my many talents, Joe. What kind of an ante does a man have to make to get in?"

"Did you ever lose at poker?"

"Friend, I'd hate to tell you how much; it grieves me to see a grown man cry. What are you thinkin' about?"

"About every two weeks, Roan Spencer used to hold a high-stake game out at the mine office. Bill Frame played, and Spencer—he owns the Golden Kate mine—and Jim Enright, who was killed on the way to town after a big winning night. A little new blood would liven up those games. Why don't you work on the idea with Bill Frame and try and sit in a few times?"

"And lose?"

"Not at first. I'm working on a notion. When I get the details straightened out, I'll let you know. It's risky, so if you want to back out——"

"Ah, that's what makes it all so interesting," O'Hagen said, and smoked his cigar.

Chapter Eleven

Roan Spencer remained late at his office. His wife was entertaining and he didn't care for that, so he invariably used it as an excuse to stay late and catch up on some of his paper work. A little before eight, he checked his watch; he was alone in the building and he went to the window and stood looking out on the town road—watching until he saw the horseman approaching. Then he went back to his desk five minutes later, Bill Frame came in and sat down.

"The building is as quiet as a tomb."

Spencer smiled. "You want someone around?"

"No, no," Frame said, settling in a chair. "What do you think ought to be done about the situation?"

"Quit?"

"Hell, no," Frame said. "That wasn't what I meant at all. I lost another man last night."

"You're bound to lose some. No one wins 'em all."

"Except Adam Collier."

"Even he can't win 'em all," Spencer repeated. "I've been doing a lot of thinking about this, Bill. I think this buttin' heads is the wrong way to go about it."

"You really think that, huh?"

"Sure. Look at it this way: when we had a marshal, we had one man standing for law and order. If he didn't play by the rules, he could be handled easily enough. But you're not dealing with one man now, Bill. No, you're not dealing with Collier alone, or Joe Beal. Kill one, or kill both, and two more men will step into their places. And the chances are that you wouldn't get away with it. It's not only the damned police department, but the people behind it, the people who like the idea of cops patrolling the streets. To get rid of them, the last thing you should use would be bullets."

"All right, what's your opinion?" Frame asked.

Spencer sat back in his chair and folded his hands. "I think the cops have made a real good impression on everyone in town. All the solid, responsible people anyway. If a cop got killed, everyone would be up in arms about it, ready to string up the killer. But if a cop was caught stealing, those same people would turn on him. You get the notion? You see how it would be? You don't kill cops, Bill. You reduce them to nothing by convincing everyone that they're a bunch of crooks, as bad as your toughs."

"Now if you ain't the sneaky one," Frame said. "It never would have occurred to me."

"Naturally," Spencer said smugly.

"But how are you going to get Beal's cops to steal?"

"People don't look too hard at faces," Spencer said. "Especially if it's dark and the lights are poor. They just see a blue uniform and shiny buttons and a badge." He leaned forward and planted his forearms on the desk. "Adam Collier is one of my best friends. I know where he bought the uniforms because he told me. I have the address right here. Now, uniforms get torn or ruined and it would be very easy to order some more. I've worded a wire. You have one of your men send it. When the order is confirmed and shipped, you make sure one of our boys covers it and picks it up. Of course, you're, doing this for Joe Beal."

"This is going to take some time. Thirty, or forty-five, days anyway."

"We can afford it. Beal has a job to do and he can't rush it. He's going to clean up the town, block by block, but he won't do it overnight. The miners aren't raising as much hell as they used to. They've been hit with night sticks and have cooled off in jail and they don't like it. All right, let him keep them in line. We'll just go undercover for awhile until it's time to move."

Bill Frame frowned. "I don't like to see money slip away."

"Now, I didn't say to quit. But don't go making the same kind of a mistake you made the other night with O'Hagen. He was a plant and you found it out, still you sent a man to his hotel. Bill, you ought to have been able to take one look at him and know that he was dangerous as hell."

"I don't make many mistakes," Frame said, his pride stung.

"You make a couple more like that," Roan Spencer said, "and I'll have to get a new manager." His voice was gentle, but the warning was there, as hard as a lancetip. "We've got a good thing going for us, Bill, and we wouldnt want to get too greedy and spoil it, would we? A man's got to know what time to play and when to quit, Bill; it's probably the most important thing he can know. Everything has to come to an end, even the gold in the mountains.

Be ready for it, boy. Be ready to take your pile and move on. Don't try to take it all. No man ever has. And no man ever will." He smiled pleasantly. "Now that makes sense, doesn't it?"

"Everything you say makes sense, Roan." Frame got up and buttoned his coat. "Let me have that telegram; I'll see that it's sent."

"Now you take it easy, huh? You come out and play poker."

"If I can find somebody," Frame said and left the mine building.

When Adam Collier left the house in the morning, his wife reminded him again about the dog for Sissy and he filed it in the back of his mind. It stayed there until late afternoon; affairs at the fire station kept him busy until it was almost time to go home to his supper.

Before he left, he remembered so he asked one of the firemen to be on the lookout for a pup, something that wouldn't grow into a horse, and went home with the promise that the word would be spread around. This promise was enough to convince Sissy that she might get a dog. Adam heard no more about it, nor did he think of it for the rest of the week.

He had a meeting in the mayor's office, and his duties at the fire station kept him busy, so when Hank Freely, the engine driver, came into his office and mentioned a puppy, Collier didn't, for a moment, know what he was talking about.

"The stationmaster's been keepin' him," Freely said. "One of the teamsters picked him up on the desert the other side of the mountains. I guess he'd be yours for the askin'."

"Thanks, Hank. I'll look into it."

Adam almost didn't bother, but he remembered in time and went to the freight depot and telegraph office. The agent, a toothless man, produced the pup—a furry ball with blue, soulful eyes and a tongue anxious to lick every face and hand in reach.

"He's yours, Adam. Glad to see him get a good home. Shame to kill a little bugger like that. Smart as a whip, too. Already broke him from p——"

"Would you take a couple of dollars for him?"

"Oh, you can have him for nothin'."

"I'll send my daughtter around to thank you for this," Collier said.

"It ain't necessary. Long as he gets a good home."

The stationmaster walked out with Collier. The sun was down and a grayness was dropping over the town. Collier tickled the pup's ears and let him gnaw on his finger.

The agent laughed and said, "Ain't named him yet. Your girl can do that, I guess." He ran a hand over his bald head. "Smart little fella. Sure is. Say, when them uniforms come in, you want me to send the freight bill to the city?"

"What uniforms?"

"Why, I guess Joe Beal ordered 'em. About the freight bill?"

"Send it to my office," Collier said and took the pup home.

When he got to his front gate, Adam whistled and Sissy and her small twin brothers came boiling out of the house. When she saw the dog, she jumped up and down and wanted to hold it; her father gave it to her and the children went on ahead into the house with their noise and clatter.

June met him and kissed him. "You're ten minutes late, but, under the circumstances, you're excused."

The evening was one of many decisions for Sissy. She had to find a place for the puppy to sleep, and make the puppy's bed, and get a bowl for the puppy to eat out of, and, of course, the puppy had to have a name. Discipline at the supper table was difficult to maintain and June excused the children early so that the pressing matters concerning the pup could be tended to.

Collier went to sit on his back porch while June did the dishes; then she came out and sat with him while he enjoyed his cigar. The noise of the stamp mill was a dull thumping in the background of the night sounds; the roar of Gold Street could not be heard at all.

Adam liked this time of the evening; the children would be put to bed soon, and the house would grow quiet. It was a time when a man could forget the troubles of the day.

The first clang of the fire bell brought his feet down off the porch railing. He kissed June quickly and ran around the house. He could see the glow of the fire against the night sky; it was across town, well down the brow of the mountainside, probably some shack going up. He heard the clang and thump of the steam pumper as he ran.

When he arrived, his firemen were already subduing the fire, unreeling leather hose, and wetting down adjoining shacks with water buckets. The heat from the shack that was on fire was charring the side of another shack, but the firemen saved it, containing the blaze which eventually razed one shack completely.

Four policemen kept the crowd back out of the firemen's way. Joe Beal arrived. Collier saw him and went over to talk to him. They walked away a bit so the shouting and noise of the pumper was less bothersome. Beal didn't have many details yet on how the fire had started, but he felt sure that it had been accidental because the owner had been found wandering around near the shack, drunk.

Collier left, walking back toward his house. He was halfway there before he remembered that he had wanted to ask Beal about ordering new uniforms. He told himself that he was going to have to get a little book to write details in; he just couldn't seem to remember them all.

Sean O'Hagen rode out to the Occidental mine for a game of poker, taking special care to arrive after the other players. He tied up alongside Fred Carlyle's buggy, went into the building, found Spencer's office with no trouble at all, and was introduced to the men he hadn't met before.

Spencer poured O'Hagen a drink and said, "Our game's dropped off since—well, it's good to sit down again with friends and pass a few hours."

"And a little money," Bill Frame said. He looked at O'Hagen and smiled. "I trust you haven't spent all your winnings."

"I only waste money on poker," O'Hagen admitted. He turned to look at Fred Carlyle who was nursing his drink and saying nothing. "Is that your rig outside? Very nice. I don't think I've ever seen one like it."

"A California maker," Carlyle said. "Well, shall we get started? I've been saving two-bit pieces for a month."

"They won't even buy cigars in this game," Spencer put in as he rubbed his hands together. "I've got luck tonight. I can feel it."

They sat down around the table, and Sean O'Hagen picked up the deck of cards.

Spencer said, "We usually cut for the deal."

"I'm going to give you a demonstration," O'Hagen said. He broke the seal on the deck, shuffled, and dealt himself four aces. For fifteen minutes he showed them a half-dozen crooked shufflles, dealing from the top, the center, and the bottom of the deck. No one could catch him.

He demonstrated crooked dealing in draw poker, stud, three-card monte, and then placed the deck of cards on the table. They watched him carefully and he spoke pleasantly. "I make my living as a gambler, gentlemen. I play any kind of card game I happen to be sitting in. If it's honest, then I play it that way. But if it's crooked, I'll take your pants before we're through."

Fred Carlyle asked, "Doesn't anyone ever catch you?"

"No," O'Hagen admitted. He picked up the cards, shuffled them, then had Spencer cut them. He had Carlyle and Frame cut them, then dealt himself four aces again. They all swore softly as he put the cards in the center of the table. "Now, if you gentlemen will name your game, we'll play."

"I've never cheated at cards in my life," Carlyle said.

Frame pursed his lips a moment. "O'Hagen, we

don't cheat, but what—ah, you see, we don't know you very well."

"If you're worried about my word, then I'll step out of the game. It's better that I do it now before someone gets shot because they have something offensive to say."

"Hell!" Spencer exclaimed. "I'll play cards with him," and he cut for the deal.

"We're all gentlemen," Carlyle declared. "Bill?"

"Mr. O'Hagen's word is good enough for me."

Frame got high card and the deal. The game was draw poker, not a fast game to win or lose on, but they had money and time. This was a five-dollar-ante game and it went along quietly, methodically, with the money changing hands, but never more than a hundred dollars at a time. Bill Frame drew so-so cards; he won a few times, lost some, and, by one o'clock, Roan Spencer was the winner by about eight hundred dollars.

A buggy came from town and a thin-faced boy brought in a tray of sandwiches and a big porcelain pot of coffee.

"You're a great host," O'Hagen said to Spencer. "I think it's almost worth losin' to you."

"Poker is a relief from the tedium of life," Spencer declared. "San Francisco is your home? I've been there a few times. A lively town."

"Growing all the time," O'Hagen said. "I jumped ship there when I was seventeen. Been there ever since. No regrets either." He took a plate, a sandwich, coffee, and sat down. Spencer was passing out cigars and O'Hagen laid his aside until he had finished eating.

"San Francisco's business opportunities have always interested me," Spencer said. "But I don't suppose you concern yourself much in that line."

"I've made a few investments," O'Hagen said modestly. "I took a half a block just off Market a few years back on a gambling debt. Sold it last year for a hundred thousand dollars. Then there were those two pieces of property on O'Farrell and one on Mission. I couldn't say what they're currently worth. Certainly a quarter of a million."

Fred Carlyle laughed. "My God, a tycoon in our midst! Now I won't feel at all badly if you lose."

"Just what brought you to Bonanza in the first place?" Bill Frame asked.

"Actually, I've been interested in the town for some time," O'Hagen admitted. "It's a long story, really, but you know how one thing leads to another. I staked a few men who came in from the diggings with color. There were a couple of brothers, Texans who'd taken a fling at the California gold fields. It wasn't much, just six hundred dollars, but they hit it rich in Columbia. Sold out to a syndicate and split it three ways, nearly four hundred thousand apiece." He shrugged. "They were going back to Texas. Cattle was really their line, so, being a gambler, I let my share ride." His smile was modest. "Right now, the Oxbow is the largest spread in Texas, and like San Francisco, it's expanding. We have graze in Montana Territory and in Wyoming. My partners are very interested in Nevada. Bonanza interested me because there's good cattleland south of here, combined with the river and the town."

"This is gold country," Frame said.

"Gold doesn't last forever," O'Hagen said. "There are plenty of towns in the California mother lode that have dried up. A boom is always followed by a bust. If you don't believe that, light a firecracker."

Chapter Twelve

As soon as school was dismissed, Sissy Collier walked three blocks over to Gold Street, traveled its fascinating, wild length, and approached the freight-yard. Wagons and mule teams filled the big yard and rough-talking teamsters spoke a language that she didn't understand at all.

Hank Freely was there; his was a familiar face—she knew the man drove the noisy fire engine and he had given her a ride on her sixth birthday. Freely saw Sissy and came over to her, squirting tobacco juice from between tight lips.

"Whatcha doin' here, Sissy?"

She peered up at this whiskered god-man who now and then descended from his high perch on the smoking, clanging, rumbling chariot. "Three weeks ago, Mr. Wigham gave daddy my puppy. I am supposed to thank him but I kept forgetting."

"He's in his office there, Sissy. You'd better take care of it and git for home. This ain't no place for you."

"Why?"

Freely fumbled for words. "Why—because there's cussin' done here."

"What's that?"

"Well, it's good you don't understand," he said, nodding and spitting.

"How old will I have to be before I can chew tobacco?"

"What? Why, girls don't chew tobacco. The idea! What ever put that notion in your head?"

"Why?"

Freely pawed a hand across his face. "If you can't ask the damndest questions!"

"Is that a cuss word?"

"What is? Oh, my! Now you just erase that from your head, you hear?" Freely took off his hat, punched it, and put it back on his head. "You go get your chore done, or I'll tell your pa on you."

Sissy went into the depot, found the agent, and thanked him for the puppy. She peppered his ear with talk about how well she fed the dog and that he had had a bath and slept in his own box and did not wet on the floor unless he got excited. She wouldn't leave until Cal Wigham told her that he, too, bathed and had a nice bed to sleep in, and that he would be glad if she came again—a small lie, but necessary when trusting brown eyes look that way at a man.

"You take a message for me to your pa?" Wigham asked. "You tell him the uniforms came in, but the freight bill was paid on them." He saw the puzzled expression on her face. "Never mind. I'll write it for you and you give him the note."

Wigham scribbled on a piece of brown paper and folded it neatly; Sissy promptly crushed it in her tight, sweaty hand and ran off. When she got home, she had chores to do: make her bed and sweep the back porch. Then she had to set the table, put out the silverware, and it was suppertime before she knew it.

Her father came home, shaved, washed, and sat down at the table. Sissy gave Adam the note from the station agent and he carefully unfolded it, trying to preserve it so that he could read it. After he had made it out, he put it aside and said, "The uniforms. I'll ask Joe Beal about them the next time I see him."

One of the boys said, "Sissy didn't come right home from school like she was supposed to."

"Oh?" Adam Collier looked at her and waited. "You went to see Mr. Wigham finally. You thanked him for the puppy and he gave you this note. That was good, but next time, don't wait so long."

"Am I going to get another dog?" Sissy asked.

"No," Collier said. "It was just an expression."

She thought this over while she chewed. "Papa, do I ask the damndest questions?"

He wasn't sure whether he should laugh or keep a straight face. "Where did you pick that up?"

She thought of Hank Freely, and to spare him, said, "At the freightyards."

June said, "Well, Adam, she's liable to hear anything there. It's not a good place for her."

"Can I chew tobacco, Papa?"

"No, I don't think that would be too ladylike," he said. "However, you have my permission to smoke a cigar any time you like."

"What a fine thing to say, Adam Collier!" June snapped. "The idea, Sissy smoking a cigar!" Then she laughed, a choked-off giggle.

"What's funny, Mama?"

"Nothing. Eat your supper." June giggled again, then started to laugh and couldn't stop. She had to leave the table.

"Your mother is a fickle woman," Adam said. "Now eat, and no more nonsense."

June came back, drying her eyes, and only little

sounds escaped her through the rest of the meal. The children were excused; they took their meat scraps out to the back porch and fed the dog.

June looked at Adam and said, "Suddenly, that was the funniest thing I'd ever imagined—a seven-year-old girl sitting on the porch with you enjoying her after-dinner cigar. Adam, what ever gives her these notions?"

"Kids are full of them."

Compared to Roan Spencer and Fred Carlyle, Able Packer didn't have much of a mine; he'd work it from spring through the fall and take out ore worth around twenty thousand which was enough to satisfy him. Most of the profits were sent east to his family to buy land and to improve the farm that had been in the family for five generations.

This was going to be his last year; the vein had all but petered out and he'd had enough of it. Packer wasn't a man who ever believed he could get rich, but he was closer than he had ever figured on coming. In all, he had sent a good thirty-five thousand back east, and banked another six in the local bank.

He could go back now, farm the rest of his life, and not have to worry about whether the crops came in good or not. He'd be a country squire, rich by local standards because he had land, money in the bank, and he could afford to have his house painted every five years.

And because he was pulling out, quitting the town, Able Packer talked more in ten minutes than he had in three years. He told Bill Frame and everyone in earshot that he was selling his claim, drawing his money out of the bank that night, buying a horse, and striking out for the railroad in Utah.

Jake Powell heard this talk. He caught Frame's quick, meaningful glance and went out to find his brother. They met in the alley, talked it over briefly, then walked up the hill toward a barn in a narrow alley. The uniforms were there.

Adam Collier was sitting up reading a book, when Phillip Clayborn, the city attorney, knocked on his front door. Collier looked at the clock; it was nearly eleven.

He opened the door and Clayborn stepped inside, taking off his hat. "Adam, I hate to disturb you, but something pretty serious has come up. May I sit down?"

"Sure, come into the parlor. June's upstairs. Can I get you a drink, Phil?"

"Thanks, no." Clayborn sat down and bit his lip. "Adam, there was another robbery tonight. A miner named Able Packer." He hesitated. "We've got some witnesses and they swear that two policemen did it."

Collier stared at Clayborn. "Phil, that's the damndest bit of nonsense I ev——"

"I'm as shocked as you are, Adam, but a dozen people saw it. At some distance, of course, but they all recognized the uniforms." He spread his hands in a helpless gesture. "The Powell brothers, Jake and Boo-Boo, both swear up and down that it was a pair of Joe Beal's men. The town will be in an uproar over this."

"I think the whole thing's insane," Collier said. "Phil, I'd stake my life on the honesty of those men. I can't make that too plain."

June Collier came down the stairs. Clayborn got up, smiled.

"Sorry to bother——" he started.

"It's all right. Are you going out, Adam?"

"Yes, and I may be very late."

"Be sure to take your key," June reminded him.

He went to the combination jail and police station with Clayborn. Joe Beal was there, pacing up and down, a cigar locked between his teeth. He looked around when Collier came in.

"It's a damned lie!" he said hotly. "Adam, you know it is."

"Yes, *I* do, but will the people in town?" Collier sat down and invited Clayborn to do the same. "I suppose the miner lost everything?"

"Cleaned out! He was going back home, giving it up. Dirty business, Adam, because a lot of people know Able Packer and like him. He is a sober, upright man." He looked at Joe Beal. "There'll have to be a hearing about this, Joe. I've already seen Judge Waller. He's going to call every officer on the force in the morning, so you might as well let them know it."

"That's fine with me," Beal said. "I don't want the citizens demanding an inquiry. You can hold it tonight if you want."

"Tomorrow's plenty of time," Clayborn said. "I'll be asking the questions and I'm going to get answers. If any of your men, off duty or on, can't account for his whereabouts at the time Able Packer was robbed, I'm going to ask for an indictment against him. It's something I'll have to do, Joe."

"By God, if you find two of my men who did this, I'll help you bring them in." Beal watched Clayborn leave, then sighed and threw his cigar butt away.

"What a rotten thing to happen. We were making a good impression, Adam. Not one officer has had to display a firearm to make an arrest. All that work down the drain."

"Well, the truth of it is bound to come out," Collier said sadly. "And Joe, if two of the men turned bad, it's best that we find it out now and do something about it."

"I just can't believe policemen did it. Damn it, I can't! I know all of them too well. Picked them too carefully."

"You don't think I want to believe it, do you? Hell, there were other witnesses besides the Powell brothers. I wouldn't take their word for anything."

"The whole thing's pretty stupid," Beal said. "It happened right on the end of Gold Street. Hell, you'd think they'd have picked an alley or something." He wiped his hand over his mouth, then shook his finger at Collier. "The thing that sticks in my craw is the uniforms. Now, who'd be stupid enough to rob somebody while in uniform?"

Collier looked at him a moment, then asked, "What did you do with those uniforms that came in?"

Beal's brow furrowed, then he looked at Adam questioningly. "What uniforms?"

"What do you mean, *what* uniforms? Hell, you ordered six uniforms—the freight agent told me a month ago. You also paid the bill the other day."

"Now wait a minute. I haven't ordered any uniforms. Each man got two and that's all. I have never picked up any uniforms at the freight office and no one from this office paid any bill. Hell, I'd have sent it to the city."

"That's what made me wonder," Collier said. "You

know, I've been meaning to ask you about those———"
He stopped talking and snapped his fingers. "All right, let's take it from the beginning. What would happen if a tough killed a cop in Bonanza?"

"We would take this town apart, board by board until we found him," Beal said. "We'd roust every whore, every cardsharp, every two-bit gunman until we got the men who did it."

"So you see that they couldn't just kill off the cops?" Collier asked. "There's too many of you, and they already figured out how it would be afterward. So what's the next thing? Discredit the police, I'd say. But to do that, they'd have to be pretty convincing, wouldn't they? Something like two cops robbing a miner in front of witnesses. Hell, they've halfway convinced Clayborn and Judge Waller and they even cast some doubts in our own minds. What do you think it'll do to the citizens?"

"Goddamn, if I don't think you're right," Beal said. He smiled as though he had never done it before and laughed softly when he lit a fresh cigar. "Adam, you know it hasn't been easy—the last hour and a half. And you're right; it did make me wonder if I'd been wrong about some of the men."

"We've got a night's work ahead of us. Before that hearing in the morning, we're going to check the story of every man on the force and line up witnesses to prove where they were. It's our only chance of getting a clean bill of health. Be sure you get the freight agent on the stand. We've got to find out who ordered those uniforms and who picked them up."

"May not be easy."

"No, but we'll surely establish that no one from the police force did it." Adam got up and turned to the door. "I'll go along Gold Street and sample the temper of the citizens."

"I'll be ready to go by midnight."

"Then I'll be back by then," Collier said and went out.

He worked his way through the crowd on Gold Street and turned into the Jackpot. One of the shotgun guards nodded toward the back and Collier went on to Frame's office. He knocked on the door.

Frame called out, "Who is it?"

There was the scraping of furniture after Collier identified himself; a moment later, Frame opened the door.

"I was checking some cash and didn't expect anyone." Frame stepped aside, then closed and locked the door. "Hell of a thing tonight, wasn't it?" he shook his head. "A bad cop will spoil the whole force. A lot of people liked Able Packer."

Collier sat down. "Some grumbling about it?"

"Grumbling? Hell, if they knew who did it, there's be a necktie party." He poured two drinks and handed one to Collier. "A case of the bad apple, Adam. We've both seen it happen before, in the army and out." Then he laughed. "Well, it's not my sweat. Sorry to see you mixed up in it. I mean, you're the mayor so it'll all come back on your head."

"Maybe we'll work it out," Collier suggested. "Suppose it wasn't anyone on the force?"

"Hell, there were witnesses!"

"The Powell brothers? Now, just how reliable are they?"

"There were others," Frame said. "Reliable people. Not pillars of the church or anything like that, but reliable men who know what they see."

"And just what did they see?"

"Two cops beat and rob Able Packer."

"Which two?"

"What difference does it make?" Frame asked hotly. "The damage has been done, hasn't it?"

Chapter Thirteen

It had not been Judge Waller's intention to hold a public hearing, but Adam Collier persuaded him that it would be wiser, even if it meant holding it in the hotel lobby which was larger than the courtroom. When news of this change got around town, a large crowd pushed into the hotel and crowded the walk and porch in front of it. Waller set up his 'bench' along the west wall and the principals were assembled. The court attendants brought quiet to the room and the hearing was opened by Judge Waller.

The city attorney asked Able Packer to step forward and be sworn in; then the miner sat down, a heavy bandage was bound around his head.

Judge Waller said, "Mr. Clayborn, in view of the fact that this is a hearing and not a trial, I have a petition from Adam Collier to act as a friend in court for the purpose of questioning witnesses. Do you object to this?"

"No, your honor."

"Very well, Mr. Clayborn. You may proceed."

The attorney nodded and faced Able Packer. "Would you describe the circumstances of your attack?"

"Ain't much to it," Packer said. "I went to the banker's house and he let me in the bank. Drew my money out, put it in my pocket, and started walkin' down the street. I was just opposite Lige Bailey's place—that's near the east end of Gold Street—when two policemen stepped out of the alley across the street and called me over." He grinned and rolled his shoulders. "I never would have gone over except that I could see the brass buttons and uniforms. Well, one asked me where I was goin' and before I could get a word out, the other banged me on the head. The next thing I knew, I woke up in Doc Ainsley's place with a sore head and empty pockets."

"How much were you carrying?"

"A little over three thousand. All gold, too."

"I have no more questions," Clayborn said. "Adam?"

"Yes." The mayor got up and stepped over to Packer. "Sitting over there is every policeman on the force. Please point to the two men who attacked you."

Packer studied the police force carefully for many minutes, then shook his head. "It was pitch dark and it happened fast. I just couldn't say." He shook his head again. "I didn't get a good look at their faces, Mr. Collier. However, I did notice that one was taller than the other."

"How tall was the shortest one?"

"No taller than me," Packer said.

"You're no more than five-feet-ten, Mr. Packer." He looked at Joe Beal. "Will the police officers please stand up? Now, Mr. Packer, you can plainly see that these are all large men, picked for their size. Not one of them is under six-feet-one. Was the taller man near that height?"

"No, I can't say that he was," Packer said. "But they sure as hell was cops. They had uniforms."

"No more questions here," Collier said. He waited until Packer stepped down, then spoke to Judge Waller. "Your honor, Joe Beal and I have been up all night, and we think we can solve this matter here and now, with your permission."

"We're interested in arriving at the truth, Mr. Collier. Go ahead, as long as Mr. Clayborn has the right to question any witnesses you wish to introduce."

"Mr. Clayborn can ask any questions he wants to," Collier said. "Your honor, Joe Beal and I investigated the whereabouts of every officer on the force at the time of the robbery and we are now prepared to produce witnesses to swear to their whereabouts. May I proceed?"

The judge nodded and Collier took over two and a half hours of the court's time, but when he was finished he had proved that no officer, on duty or off, could have taken part in the robbery; they were all accounted for: where they were, what they were doing; they were vouched for by substantial citizens whom no one in their right mind would have doubted.

Then Collier patiently, piece by piece, produced evidence to prove that someone other than a city employee or official had ordered six police uniforms and picked them up at the freight depot and paid the bill for them. The freight agent could not identify the man, but he was positive that it had not been one of the policemen.

"Your honor," Collier said, "it is clear to me that there is a plot underfoot to discredit the law enforcement agency in Bonanza. I believe we have clearly proved that no individual officer on the force could have been in two places at the same time; therefore, he could not have been involved in

the robbery. Secondly, we have proved that persons
unknown purchased, in the city's name, six police
uniforms and intends to put them to no good purpose. I suggest, your honor, that the robbers intended solely to discredit the force by committing
this robbery before witnesses."

Waller glanced at Clayborn. "Have you a rebuttal
to this?"

Clayborn stood up, saying, "I believe the points
are well taken and I concur with them."

"Then it is my opinion," Waller said, "that the police force is innocent of all suspicion. Chief Beal, I in-
struct you to investigate this matter with every
means at your disposal and bring the matter to a
close. Nothing would please me more than to see
the guilty parties before my bench."

"I think you can count on it," Beal said.

While the townspeople were filing out, Clyde
Meers came over to Collier. Meers was folding his
notes and stuffing them into his pocket. "I'll have a
lively edition this time," he said. "You may have
cleared yourself, but it won't stop talk. A lot of people won't think it out and they'll say you pulled a
sneaky."

"I can't help that," Collier said. "But we've got
something to work on now."

"So have they. Six uniforms." Meers winked and
went out.

Collier went to Beal's office and found him there;
he hauled a chair around and sat down, facing Beal.
"Let's do some adding," he invited. "I'm convinced
that the Powell brothers are two of the toughs."

"Right! But what charge can we arrest them on?"

Beal gnawed on his cigar. "They didn't get called as witnesses; I think they were disappointed."

"That BooBoo's not all there," Collier said. "He was hurt in a mine explosion about ten years ago and hasn't been right since."

"So?"

"So I've been thinking about him and the way he acted that day he thought Malloy was going to beat out my brains."

"Keep going," Beal encouraged Collier. "My ticket takes me to the end of the line."

"Well, it wouldn't be hard to sucker BooBoo into something," Collier said. "I think if he was worked on a little, he'd talk."

"Pound on him?" Beal asked. "The idea's good, but I'm against it. You pound on him, but where does it stop?"

"If he had all his marbles, maybe, but with him the way he is, you could work on him by using his limited intel——"

Beal smiled. "That, I'm not against. But how do you approach a guy like that? Not you or me. Certainly, not a cop."

"There's one man who goes all over town and nobody thinks a thing of it. Clyde Meers."

"Yes, that's right. He could talk to BooBoo without making him suspicious. You want me to get Meers? I saw him heading for his office."

"Let's both go talk to him," Collier suggested and they went out and down the street.

Clyde Meers usually did his drinking alone, in private, but he was in and out of saloons so often that his lounging against the bar attracted no attention or comment. He had to wait half an evening before he caught BooBoo Powell alone, and then Meers sidled up to him as though by accident; he finally 'saw' BooBoo and bought him a drink.

"You seen any good fights lately?" Meers asked.

"Naw, the police stopped the fightin' on the streets. Why?" He watched Meers with intent, watery eyes, and that vacant attention the feeble-minded place on everything.

"Oh, I've got a bit of a problem," Meers admitted.

He said no more. Eventually, BooBoo picked it up. "I like a good fight. When I watch a good fight, it's like it was me there, just beatin' up on everybody."

"A way for you to get even, huh?" Meers smiled. "Know how that is, BooBoo. They've dealt me a lot of dirt in my life, too." He refilled the glasses. "You wouldn't know where two men could have it out, would you? Some place where the police wouldn't bother them?"

"Is there goin' to be a fight?"

Meers leaned close and became very confidential. "Listen, BooBoo, there's a fight cooking like you've never seen before. A couple of gentlemen, mind you, got on to arguing and, before you know it, one had challenged the other. A duel to the finish."

"Damn, I'd like to see that. It's always better when someone gets killed. I seen one once where a fella had both eyes tore out; it was the best fight I ever saw."

"That'd be nothin' compared to this one," Meers confided. "You know about the code of duels, Boo-Boo? Well, the challenged party has the choice of weapons, you know."

"Damn, knives, huh?"

"Worse. Razor-sharp hatchets in a dark room." He watched BooBoo's eyes get round and excited. "I'm supposed to arrange it, but I just don't know where to turn. It's got got to be a pitch-black room with no windows. And it's got to be where the police won't interfere." He shook his head. "There's just some things a man can't do, I guess."

"I'd sure like to see that room afterward," BooBoo said. "I sure would."

"You might as well forget it," Meers advised. "But I'd give a hundred dollars if I could find a place— somewhere that isn't going to be found by the police."

"I know a place."

"Aw, you don't!"

"Do so. Only me and two others know about it." He took Meers by the sleeve. "You let me see it afterward and I'll show you this place."

"By golly," Meers said, "I'm inclined to take you up on that. But you're not joshing me, are you, BooBoo?"

"Sure ain't. You want to see it?"

"Any time."

"I'll take you there now. Meet me on the west corner of Gold in fifteen minutes. But don't you tell anybody. If Jake found out, he'd beat my head off."

"Not a word," Meers promised; he paid for the drinks and went out. He walked down to the west corner of Gold Street and watched the traffic, then someone touched him on the elbow and he jumped. BooBoo was standing in the deep shadows; he nodded for Meers to follow him.

To keep out of sight, they took the alleys and worked their way up the tiered side of the mountain to the red light district—dark, curtained houses with a steady stream of customers coming and going.

Powell led Meers into a narrow alley, then they worked their way along through a narrow gap between buildings until they came to a door. BooBoo produced a key and chuckled. "Sneaked this from Jake's pocket. I'll have to put it right back."

BooBoo fitted it to the lock, opened the door and they stepped inside. After a moment of fumbling, he found the lamp and lit it. The room was long and narrow, with a steel cage at one end and one other door.

BooBoo said, "Jake and I built this ourselves." He pointed to the other door. "That goes into a closet. You open the closet door from the building side and you can't tell that one's even there."

"You say no one knows this room is here?"

"Just three people. Not even Fat Ella who runs this place."

"Now, by golly, I believe this will do." Meers clapped BooBoo on the shoulder. "I'll set it up for tomorrow night if you can get the key again. Say around midnight?"

"I'll get the key."

"And I'll have a hundred dollars for you."

"I don't care about the money. There'll be lots of blood, won't they?"

"Lots of blood," Meers said. He went outside while Powell blew out the lamp and locked the door. They said goodbye in the alley and BooBoo Powell went back to Gold Street while Meers cut through the alleys to Joe Beal's office.

The chief wasn't there; the officer on duty said he had gone to Collier's. Meers thanked him and hurried out. He found both the men on the front porch, talking softly and smoking cigars.

When Meers sat down, Beal asked, "Well, did you see BooBoo?"

"Yes. It worked out better than I thought."

"Well, as long as you can get him someplace quiet where he can be grabbed without attracting attention——"

"He showed me just the place," Meers said. "I don't know what to make of it, but I think you both ought to see it. Can either of you pick a lock?"

"If it's not too complicated," Beal said, getting up. He looked at Meers, standing to one side so the light coming through the lace curtains fell on him. "You sound kind of excited?"

"Wait until you see this place," Meers said. "It gives a man the creeps, drunk or sober."

"What does?" Collier asked.

"Oh, an outside secret entrance and another through a closet. And that damned steel cage at one end. Like they kept some wild animal there."

For a moment, Beal and Collier looked at each other, then Beal said, "I guess you've hit on it, Clyde. They do keep an animal in that cage."

Chapter Fourteen

Joe Beal tried to pick the lock; but after fifteen minutes, he gave up and brought out a ring of skeleton keys; he managed to get one to work and opened the door inward. Meers found the lamp and lit it while Collier closed the door. The three men stood there, looking around the room.

There was the table and chair and the lamps on standards with the strong reflectors that Beal had described—and the cage. It was obvious to Collier, after inspecting the room, just how he had missed finding it when he had made his detailed fire inspection months before. The room was no more than six-feet wide, but it was long, running half the length of the house.

"Let's get out of here," Beal said. "Disturb nothing." He waved them out, then blew out the lamp and closed and locked the door. They moved sideways between the buildings to the alley, had a look in both directions, then took a careful route back to his office.

"BooBoo told me that he and his brother built that room," Meers said. "He also mentioned several times that only three men knew of its existence. Since we know the identity of two———"

"And I've met the third man," Beal said, "although I can't identify him."

Meers explained how he was going to meet Boo-Boo Powell the following night.

Beal said, "That's the place to take him then. He'll come alone and expect to meet you and two other men. I think Malloy and his partner can handle this. We can keep him out at the ranch if the bank hasn't sold it for back taxes."

"I can check on that in the morning," Collier said. "But we took a six-month lease, Joe, and we've got a while to go on it. We'll have to bring Clayborn in on this the minute we find out anything definite."

"Let's not get in a hurry about that," Meers said. "The man is a refined gentlemen and all that, but he's liable to put his foot down about proper questioning procedure."

"Now, we're not going to beat Powell," Beal said. "Collier and I agreed on that already."

"Well, he won't talk unless you do," Meers said. "Stupid, yes, but a coward, no. However, there are always things every man is afraid of. Take ourselves, for instance. Let's confess our own private fears. Adam?"

"Snakes," Collier said. "They really get to me. I can think about 'em and break out in a cold sweat."

"Then if I knew that about you," Meers pointed out, "I'd figure out some fiendish way to use that fear. Perhaps I'd put you in a dark, locked room with a diamondback rattler."

"Good lord, Clyde!" Beal said. "We're policemen, not Apaches."

Meers looked at him and smiled. "All right, what's your fear?"

Beal acted as though he didn't want to say, then he said, "I think it's smothering, with my hands and feet tied so I can't help myself, and a gag in my mouth so that I can't breathe." He gave a shudder. "I could take anything but that."

"I'd have you sewn up in a heavy sack," Meers declared. "You see how simple it all is? For myself, I've always had a fear of fire, of catching my clothes and hair afire and burning. What a hell of a way to go!" He looked from one to the other. "BooBoo Powell was once a man like us, intelligent, strong. But he had an accident. He was buried alive in a mine cave-in for nearly nine hours; when they dug him out he was a raving maniac. It was a year before he could feed himself and remember to stop messing his pants. In time, he got a little better, but he'll never be all right." He stopped talking and smiled. "Now, I know how to break BooBoo Powell. By the time I got finished with him, he'd tell me the name of the constellations in the heavens and recite for me the history of the Greek gods."

"Meers, you're a damned Indian," Joe Beal said. "We can't treat people like that, no matter how much it means to us. Where would it stop? Pretty soon we'd be beating every prisoner that was brought in here." He held up his hand when Meers opened his mouth to object. "Don't tell me that it wouldn't be that way; I've seen it myself. Listen, the only chance law has to survive is to create an equality that everyone understands and trusts. The worst type of criminal will have to finally understand that he won't be beaten or abused, but punished only in accordance with whatever decision a court of law hands down."

"Where the hell did you leave your congregation? Joe, these are tough times. We're trying to break a gang that will stop at nothing."

"Then it's to our credit if we break it with routine police methods," Beal insisted.

"Adam, you ought to fire him—for the time being, anyway."

"I've got to go along with him," Collier said. "But there's nothing to stop us from doing it with talk." He got up and gave Clyde Meers a slap on the shoulder. "Joe will work out the arrangements for the arrest. You play it his way, understand?"

"Oh, hell, yes," Meers said, sighing heavily. "By God, you'll have me swore off drink before you're through."

"Water wouldn't hurt you," Collier said as he left for home.

June was waiting up; she had baked a pie and had a pot of coffee on. They sat in the parlor, eating, enjoying the little quiet they had together.

"I was talking to Mrs. Fillmore down the street today," June said. "There's still talk around town about the policemen who robbed Mr. Packer."

"That's to be expected. We may catch the real criminals though."

She looked at him quickly. "Do you have something to go on?" He shrugged and she didn't press him further; he wasn't a man who liked to be pushed when he didn't want to move. "Sean O'Hagen came around this evening, but you'd gone out. He promised to drop back." She turned her head and looked at the hall clock. "It's nearly eleven-thirty."

"Doesn't that thing chime anymore?"

"We'll have to get it fixed. The children were playing and Sissy bumped it; a spring went, boooiiing, and it never chimed again."

"Springs do go like that sometimes," he said.

Then he got up when he heard the gate open and close. He met O'Hagen at the door and asked him in for pie and coffee.

"I've been playing poker, Adam. Very interesting fellows."

"Yeah, they're all right. I've known them for some time."

O'Hagen smiled and shook his head. "I said they were interesting, not 'all right.' Fred Carlyle is a coaster. By that, I mean, he goes along with the tide. He doesn't get in too deep. Not in anything." He glanced at June. "This is fine pie. Excellent."

"I do believe you mean that, Mr. O'Hagen."

"Honesty gets me in trouble sometimes," he admitted. "About Bill Frame. He's a crook."

"Bill and I served together for years and I'd back him——"

"You'd lose," O'Hagen said gently. "He deals sharp and he lies." He waited for the thunder to sound; it was in Collier's face. "I knew you wouldn't like this, but the man's dishonest."

"How do you know that?"

"By the way he plays cards. You can learn a lot about a man playing cards."

"I suppose you have some sage opinion about Roan Spencer?"

"Yes, he's as dishonest as Frame. And he can't stand to lose, not even a fifty-dollar pot."

"Why, Roan's a wealthy man!"

"Sure, but that doesn't keep a man from being greedy." O'Hagen took the last bite of his pie and got up. "I've disturbed you enough. I'm sorry, but I have to call the hand the way I see it."

"In this, you're wrong," Collier said. "Sean, you'll have to prove it to me."

"Tomorrow night then? Spencer wants to play and I told him I thought I could bring in some new blood."

"All right," Collier said. "About nine? We'll ride out together."

"I'll meet you at the edge of town then," O'Hagen said. "Good night, ma'am."

After O'Hagen had left, Collier came back from the porch and sat down. "I'm trying not to get mad, June. I'm trying not to let friendship interfere with good sense."

"Adam, he wasn't lying." She said it very quietly and he looked at her. She put her cup down and folded her hands. "I've never liked to take any credit for woman's intuition, but I think there's something to it, Adam. I want you to think back carefully and ask yourself just how many times Bill has ever come here."

"Why, I don't think he's ever been in the house," Collier said. "What of it?"

"And when you were in the army, how many times did he come to our quarters? I mean, past the door. I can answer for you. Not once. And here you always meet him at the sutlers or the stables or on Gold Street or in his saloon. That's inclined to make a woman suspicious, Adam."

"Of what?"

She shrugged. "I don't know. If I knew, I'd have told you a long time ago. It was just a feeling and it really sounds pretty silly when you come right out and talk about it. But you have to ask yourself,

Adam: just what does Sean O'Hagen have to gain by lying to you?"

"I have been asking," Collier said. "Maybe I should have played poker with Bill and Roan before."

Other than mentioning to Joe Beal that he was going out to Roan Spencer's mine, Collier kept the facts of the poker game to himself; he found it difficult to put aside past loyalties and he knew that if he ever had to make a decision regarding either man that he would lean over backward to be tolerant. This wasn't a good way to be; a man ought to go by the facts and let nothing stand in his way. Still, he had to choose a side, had to believe one way or another, just as he had believed that none of the policemen had been guilty of robbery.

He met O'Hagen at the end of Gold Street and they rode out to the mine together. The heat of the day had vanished and a breeze was coming up. There was little talk between them; they seemed content to enjoy the evening and their own thoughts.

Carlyle's buggy and Frame's horse were already there when they arrived; they dismounted, tied up, and went in. Roan Spencer was pouring drinks; he looked up in surprise when Collier stepped into the room.

"By golly, I didn't know you had a thirst for poker," Spencer said. He smiled and handed Collier a glass. "Cigars are on the table. I like to be a good host."

"I thought marriage weaned you from cards, Adam," Frame said, watching Collier over the rim of his glass.

"O'Hagen said there was some easy money here."
They all laughed.

"Not the way we play," Spencer said. He rubbed his hands together. "Shall we get started? The sooner we slay the lambs, the better."

Collier played a waiting game for an hour; he was a smooth, quiet player who handled his cards intelligently and drew no attention to himself. Then he deliberately drew blood from Roan Spencer and Bill Frame by staying in, playing it out, riding the raises that Spencer threw at Frame. Collier let them duel, stayed with them, shoved his money in until Spencer finally called.

"Three little old ladies," Spencer said and reached for the pot.

Frame held up his hands. "Aces." He made a fan of three cards.

"I've got two pair," Collier said quietly. "All threes."

Carlyle was out; he'd dropped out some time before and he watched this carefully, a thin smile on his face, his eyes flicking from Spencer to Frame and then to Collier.

Spencer stared at the cards. "Where the hell did those come from?"

"I got them on the deal," Collier said. He looked across at Fred Carlyle. "He gave them to me, then Bill opened, and I drew one card."

"Then why the hell didn't you raise and let a man know you had a hand?" Spencer asked hotly.

"That's not the way the game is played. Besides, you were after Bill, not me." He reached out and pulled in fifteen hundred dollars. "Thank you for this contribution, gentlemen. I always like to take money from men who can afford it."

"I'll be a sonofabitch if I like it," Spencer said and got up to get a drink.

Bill Frame was smiling around his cigar, but his eyes were almost squinted shut as he watched Collier neatly stack the money. "I had forgotten your tactics, Adam. My fault. Flank 'em and hit 'em hard—it was always that way, wasn't it?"

"It sure worked for J.E.B. Stuart."

Spencer came back and sat down, slapping a new deck on the table. "Maybe this will change my luck. Deal, Bill." He sat there, rolling his cigar from one corner of his mouth to the other, impatiently tapping his fingers on the green cover while the cards slapped down.

The men picked up their cards, glanced at them, and O'Hagen held up his fingers for two. Carlyle took three and Collier one.

Spencer said, "Not again!" He held up a finger.

Bill Frame took two, studied his hand briefly, then chucked it.

They sweetened the ante. Carlyle opened for ten dollars and Spencer made some derisive remark about cheap skates. Since Frame had thrown in his hand, he leaned over to see what Spencer had.

"I think I'll raise this a hundred dollars," Spencer said.

Carlyle looked around, then rolled his thin shoulders. "Call and raise a hundred."

The betting went around and Spencer tossed down his hand and got up to get another drink. Frame picked up the deck of cards, including his own discards, and placed them to one side.

When Spencer came back and sat down, he reached out to pick up his cards, stopping when O'Hagen said, "Before you play those cards, Mr. Spencer, let me make a little side bet with Mr. Collier that they are queens or higher, and four of a kind."

"What the hell are you saying?" Spencer asked.

"That the hand you laid down on the table when you went to fill your glass is now in the deck, and that Mr. Frame's hand, which was a winner, but which he discarded, is now face down on the table. If you gentlemen want to cheat at cards, you'll have to do better than that." He rested his hands flat on the table and watched the color drain from Spencer's face.

Collier wondered why Spencer didn't hit Bill Frame; an innocent man would have. He shuttled his glance between them and knew that Sean O'Hagen was right, and that he'd proved it the hard way.

"You looked at your hand too long, Mr. Spencer; a man will do that when he's trying to make something out of the mess he's been dealt. If you'd drawn a winner, a glance would have been enough." He looked at Bill Frame. "And you threw your hand away with no more than a glance."

"I think fast," Frame said.

"And I'm going to give you a chance to think fast now," O'Hagen said gently.

"I'm not armed," Frame said.

"That's a lie! You wouldn't come from town without protection. No man in his right mind would." He slashed out with his hand and ripped open Frame's coat; the butt of his revolver which rested in a shoulder holster, was visible.

Then O'Hagen hunched his right shoulder; there

was the sound of a spring catch releasing and a small two-barreled .44 popped into his palm. "I carry one myself, in addition to a shotgun on the saddle." He looked from Frame to Spencer and back. "I think I've played enough poker with you gentlemen. In fact, I think this terminates any other business we might have had."

Fred Carlyle said, "This is hard for me to believe, Roan. Turn up your cards and make a liar of him." He waited but Spencer didn't move. Then Carlyle reached out to turn the cards face up, but Spencer slapped his hand down on them.

"You want to see these, you pay for it!"

"We've paid," Collier said. "Turn them over, Roan, or I'll do it for you."

Spencer tried to stare him down but failed; he flipped the cards over, scattering them, but they could all count four kings. He took his glass and got up, speaking with his back to them. "Go on, get out of here."

Collier pocketed his money; he was the big winner.

Bill Frame had remained seated. He said, "Adam, I'd hate to think that a card game could wipe out all the years we've——"

"I found out something about you that I didn't know," Collier said. "Now I'm wondering what else there is that I don't know."

He turned, went outside, and stood by his horse. It was cool enough to need a coat so he put his on, then O'Hagen came out and untied and climbed into the saddle.

They rode back together. Finally O'Hagen said, "It was no pleasure for me; I want you to believe that."

"I know. But I sure didn't see the switch."

"Neither did I," O'Hagen said. He met Collier's startled eyes with a smile. "But I'd been watching Spencer; it was a natural setup. That and the way they looked at their cards. So I bluffed."

"That was dangerous."

"They're both dangerous men," O'Hagen said and let it go at that.

The fact that Adam got home before midnight surprised June Collier; she had the lamp at the bedside turned down and when he came into the room, she reached up and raised the wick.

"When a man comes home from a poker game at this hour," she said, "it is probably because he ran out of money."

"No, I won about fifteen hundred," Adam said.

She studied his expression and the tone of his voice. "O'Hagen was right, wasn't he?" Then she patted the bed beside her. "Sit down, Adam."

"No, I'm going to go uptown to see if I can find Joe Beal." He went to the closet and got his shotgun. "Go to sleep. I don't know when I'll be back." He bent and kissed her, then turned down the lamp. He went down the stairs and out to his front gate. As he turned to close it, he looked up and saw two men walking toward him. He was just starting to shift the shotgun when one of the men ran his night stick along the pickets of a fence and Collier relaxed.

It almost cost him his life.

The two men were within six feet of him before he realized that he'd been pulled into a false sense of security, just like Able Packer. One of the men swung his night stick and Collier instinctively flung up an arm to ward off the blow. He heard the bones in his forearm snap. The force of it swung him half around; he pressed the muzzle of the shotgun against the chest of the second man and pulled the trigger.

The charge knocked the man flat and Collier whirled away. A whirling night stick splintered support and pickets from his fence, then the first man turned and started to run. Collier let him get four jumps down the street before he gave him the second barrel high in the back. The man pitched forward, rolled, and lay still.

In his house, June was turning on lamps and Adam yelled, "Stay inside! Do you hear, June? Stay inside!"

His left arm was completely dead; he could not move his fingers at all. So he locked the barrel of the shotgun between his knees, broke it open, fished in his pocket for two fresh shells and snapped it closed.

The shots had awakened the neighborhood and he knew they carried to the fringes of Gold Street. Collier was beginning to feel pain now; he felt sick and his legs shook; he wondered if he were going to fall. There were some men running down the street, yelling questions at each other, trying to locate the source of the shooting.

Collier leaned against the fence and yelled, "That's far enough! Identify yourself!"

"Sanderson! Police officer! Riley is with me!" He spoke in a lower tone. "The rest of you stand back until we see what's going on." He raised his voice again. "Sing out down there! Identify yourself in the name of the law!"

Collier thought he recognized the voice and wiped a match aflame as the two policemen came on. They carried tin lanterns and lit them, hanging them on the fence. Riley went back to keep the crowd away as Sanderson looked at the dead men.

Sanderson straightened and said, "I've never seen either of them before. Are you hurt, Mr. Collier?"

"I think my arm's broken." He was breathing heavily and his head was beginning to spin. "If you'll send for the doctor, I think I'll go inside." He stumbled to the gate, opened it, and would have fallen if Sanderson hadn't caught him and supported him into the house.

Collier remembered opening the gate and that was all until he opened his eyes and found himself in bed with his left arm in a heavy splint and wrapping. Dr. Stover was closing his bag and Joe Beal was leaning against the wall by the door. June was near him, her hand wiping his forehead with a damp cloth.

Downstairs, the hall clock chimed three o'clock.

Collier frowned and said, "I thought that thing was broken."

"It started working after supper," June explained.

Stover moved over to the bed and felt Collier's pulse. "Strong as an ox. You can get out of bed tomorrow if you feel like it."

"I fell for a sucker trick," Adam said. "Stupid as hell, wasn't it?"

"The same one Able Packer fell for," Beal put in. "We got Able out of bed; once he saw the two men he recognized them. Pretty bold, I'd say, going after you that way. It means they're scared."

"I'll look in on you tomorrow," Stover said, picking up his bag. June started to turn to the door, but Stover shook his head. "I'll show myself out. Good night."

After the doctor had gone down the stairs, Beal said, "We arrested BooBoo Powell and got him out of town. No trouble at all. Well, he gave Malloy a bit of a fight—but who can fight that man? It's like kicking a locomotive because it whistled at you."

"Pull up a chair and sit down," Collier invited. He stirred in bed and was instantly sorry because shooting pains traveled all the way to his shoulder. "I played poker tonight, Joe."

"Sean told me. It makes a man wonder, doesn't it?"

"Wonder about what?"

Beal shrugged and studied his hands. "A man lies about one thing, he'll lie about another."

"Get to your point."

"I think you know my point."

"Now I don't connect what happened at Spencer's with my being jumped."

"Why not?" Beal asked gently. "If Roan or Bill left right after you and Sean, they'd have had time to sick these toughs on you."

"You know what you're really saying? You're telling me that Bill or Roan are right in the middle of this other thing."

"That's right," Beal admitted. "I suspect them and, until I find out differently, I'll go on suspecting them. That's part of my job, Adam."

"I won't argue that, but you ask questions before you mention this to anyone," Collier advised. "And I'll tell you right out that I'm just as anxious to prove them as innocent as we proved the cops on your force are."

"Sure. Hell, I'd rather find them innocent myself." Beal rubbed his knees as he turned something over in his mind. "How far would you go to prove this one way or another, Adam?"

"To the end of the line. Suspicions have been raised in my mind and I don't like it at all."

"Then I'll see what can be worked out in a few days," Beal promised. "Get some sleep. Tomorrow afternoon, we'll go out to the ranch, if you feel up to it."

June went down with the marshal and locked the door after he went out. Then she came back with a glass of water and emptied a paper envelope into it. "Now you drink this and you'll sleep until noon."

"Suppose I want to wake up at eleven?"

"Never mind."

She gently raised his head and he drank nearly all the medicine. Then Adam sighed and let his head sink back into the pillow.

June sat on the edge of his bed. "Just what did you think you were going to do when you started to run out of the house?"

"Oh," she said, "I think I was afraid someone would stomp my flower bed. You know how often I have to water them."

"And I thought you were concerned about me," Adam said, with a tone of exaggerated disappointment. The pain was slacking off in his arm and he felt very drowsy. She turned down the lamp by the bedside and took her pillow and an extra blanket from the closet.

When she kissed him and started to leave, he could not summon the energy to say good night.

* * *

Adam did not sleep until noon, not by ten minutes. He had already dressed himself and was coming down the stairs before June heard him; by then it was too late to stop him. She came from the kitchen, wiping her hands on her apron.

"I don't suppose," she said, "that telling you that I think this is very foolish would do any good?"

"Not a particle. Any coffee? Maybe some eggs? A little bacon? A couple of slices of bread? Pancakes? Leftover pie?"

She smiled and cocked her head to one side. "Are you hungry?"

He went with her to the kitchen and she fixed a meal for him, then sat down across from him while he ate. He had put his shirt over one shoulder and around his broken arm, buttoning it so that the arm was against his body, protected.

"Has Joe been around yet?"

"No. Adam, you're not going out to that ranch, are you? You won't be back until after ten o'clock."

He raised his eyebrows and smiled. "Did you have something special planned for me tonight?"

"Oh, now be serious." She fought back a smile.

"It's my arm that's broken, you know, not———"

"All right now!" June wasn't angry with him, but she got up and bustled about a little. Then she came back and put her arm around him and kissed him. "You're a bad boy—I'm happy to say. Now eat the meal you wanted."

Afterward, he went to his front porch to sit; his arm throbbed, but he'd endured things like this before and each day would bring a little less discomfort; in two months, it wouldn't hurt at all.

Clyde Meers came down the street with his mincing gait as though he had to pick each step carefully. Collier, watching him come on, supposed that the man had been drunk so many times that the habit of moving carefully was deeply ingrained.

Meers sat down on the step where there was good shade and wiped his face with a large handkerchief. "I don't see why," Meers said, "in consideration for an older man, you can't wait until you get to Gold Street before shooting it out with ruffians. It would save me a good deal of walking in this unbearable heat." He looked at Collier's splinted arm bulging under his shirt. "I hope that isn't serious. Stover won't tell a man a damned thing, you know. Afraid he'll reveal his own ignorance." He looked up, smiling as June came out with a pitcher of tea. "Just what I hate most," he said, taking a glass. "But I can pretend that it's whiskey; such is the power of my mind. Virtually limitless, I assure you, trained that way by long practice and devotion to the mystic arts of the inscrutable east."

"Clyde Meers, you're a terrible man, but I like you," June said.

Meers offered her a toast. "My dear woman, if there should ever come a day when you tire of this oaf, and seek solace with a gentleman of letters, please——"

"I know. Call you at any hour of the day or night," she said.

"Exactly," Meers said, then drank some of his tea. "My, but that's abominable stuff. Do people really drink this for pleasure?"

"You'll drink every bit of it," June insisted.

"He really likes it," Collier said. "Confess it, Clyde."

"Well, I wouldn't want it to get around, but it does

quench the thirst. Leave the pitcher." He smiled as she went inside, then Collier's children came out and sat on the porch. Sissy had her pup on a leash. The boys sat beside her and they all studied Meers intently. Since he was a man unaccustomed to the curiosity of children, he began to feel ill at ease.

Adam said, "Sissy, why don't you go and play some place? Mr. Meers and I want to talk."

"We won't interrupt, Papa."

"Go before I swat you!"

They scampered off the porch and ran down the street, all noise and stamping feet; the pup barked and ran along beside them.

Meers said, "I've often thought of marriage and children, and then I think of suicide and give up the whole idea." He drank his tea and refilled his glass. "Joe mentioned a poker game last night." His glance was veiled, but his tone was sympathetic. "A long time ago I came to the conclusion that it's hard to tell about people. And most of the time you can't really tell anything at all."

"I'll have to have proof, Clyde. Real proof."

"Of course. I spent the night in the country. Fresh air and no noise. Couldn't sleep a wink. BooBoo Powell is scared. No one's told him why he's been arrested. He keeps yelling for his brother."

"I blame him the least," Adam Collier said. "Hell, he doesn't know what he's doing half the time. He's had his screws knocked loose."

"We're working kind of a game with BooBoo. Malloy and Childs are pretty gruff with him. It was my idea, so don't blame Beal. I'm trying to go along with you, Adam."

"Don't knock him around."

Meers shook his head. "Nothing like that. But I want BooBoo to get the notion planted in his head that Malloy and Childs are his enemies and that I'm his friend. For everything they do that worries him, I do something to ease his mind. I want him to turn to me, like I was a father confessor." He took out his pocket watch. "I'm supposed to meet Phillip Clayborn here. He'll have his buggy and I thought you might like to drive out with us. Clayborn is an ass, just like you and Beal, but there's nothing to do but humor you all along. He says that BooBoo will have to volunteer any confession we get and that Judge Waller will throw it out of court if we force one out of him." He made a disgusted sound with his lips. "Of course, you're all right, but you know me, Adam—I hate to admit anyone has any brains." He raised his glass in salute. "My compliments in reducing the undesirable population of Bonanza by two. I trust you'll bag the limit? I loathe a man who'll shoot only a pair for mounting."

Chapter Fifteen

The ranch where BooBoo Powell was being held had originally been leased by Adam Collier as a matter of speculation. It was in a good location, with a good well and a creek, but two farmers had gone broke trying to raise grain and vegetables on it when it clearly was suitable only for cattle. The bank held the paper on the place and Collier took a six-month lease by paying the interest on the loan.

To rid the place of some ramshackle buildings, Collier had used it to train his firemen, setting fire to the buildings piece by piece so the men could gain experience with tinderboxes that went up like struck matches. When the police unit was formed, the ranch, with its rebuilt buildings, had made an ideal training site.

Meers and Collier rode out in Phillip Clayborn's buggy. Joe Beal's horse was tied near the porch, where broad branches of a valley oak provided shade. Malloy was on duty. He was in the kitchen talking to Beal when Meers halted the team and the policemen came out as the men were dismounting.

"How's our rabbit?" Meers asked dryly.

"Worried," Beal said. "Scared and trying not to show it."

The ranch house was a solid adobe building in

good condition; it was dim and cool inside and Beal jerked his thumb toward the storeroom in the back.

"It was the only room with no windows and only one door," Beal explained. "No one's questioned him or bothered him, except Childs and Malloy. He won't tell them anything."

"It's about time I worked my persuasive charms," Meers said. "Phillip, you understand how this is. Wouldn't you like to be your old evil self?"

Clayborn nodded and Malloy unlocked the door.

Powell was stretched out on a cot; he came awake when the door opened and stood with his back to the wall, crowded into a corner from which he could defend himself.

Meers said, "Malloy, leave this door open. The poor man doesn't have any light in here." He looked at Powell. "How are they treating you, BooBoo? Clayborn, this is terrible, keeping a man locked up in a room without windows. I'm going to write an article about it in my paper." He walked up to Powell and took him gently by the arm. "Sit down, man. I'm not going to let anyone hurt you. Why, it was only today that I found out you'd been arrested, and then I had to pry it out of the police. I saw Jake and he's worried about you. That's why I started asking around, and when no one knew anything, I went to Joe Beal. We just can't have our citizens disappearing, you know."

"Where's Jake?" BooBoo asked.

"We'll see that he gets invited to the hanging," Clayborn said.

BooBoo's eyes darted to him. "What hangin'? Me? I ain't done a thing."

"Now don't excite yourself," Meers said soothingly. "Clayborn, you shouldn't say things like that.

It doesn't matter if he killed Jim Enright or not; he still has ri——"

"Me?" Powell asked. "I didn't kill nobody." He jumped to his feet again and backed into the corner. "What ya sayin'? Who says I did?"

Clayborn was very casual. "Now I don't see any sense in lying about it, BooBoo. You certainly fit the description of the man."

"Wha—what you mean? Nobody saw it!"

"How can you be sure of that?" Clayborn asked. "Were you alone? Did you kill him by yourself, Boo-Boo?"

"Why don't you just ask him one question at a time?" Meers said testily. "BooBoo and I are friends and I don't like to see him treated this way."

Powell darted his eyes from one to the other. "Meers, help me! Tell Jake I'm here! Find Jake and tell him and he'll get me out!"

"Of course, I will," Meers said gently. "And I'll come back and see you, BooBoo. If they beat you or starve you or anything like that, I'll see that justice is done."

"What good's that gonna do me?"

"The principle of the thing," Meers said and stepped to the door.

Clayborn gave Powell a dark study, then stepped out, and the door started to close. Then Adam Collier put out his hand and stopped it; he came in and sat down on Powell's bunk.

"You've got yourself in some trouble, BooBoo."

"I just don't understand it."

"Maybe I can explain it to you," Collier said. "We know you're part of the gang of toughs that beat and rob people in town."

"How—do you know that?"

"Because you knew where the secret room was. That's where the leader of the toughs meets people. Isn't that right, BooBoo?"

"I don't know what it's used for."

"Sure you do. You and Jake built it and you're both members of the gang. You wear matches in your hatbands, don't you? That's the sign that you're in the gang."

The prisoner's eyes got round. "How did you know that?"

Collier smiled pleasantly. "Why, every policeman in town knows it, BooBoo. That's why there haven't been any beatings and robberies, because the police keep a close eye on these men with matches in their hatbands. That's why when Jake whistles and gives the signal——"

"He don't whistle," BooBoo said quickly.

"Then how does he do it? Wiggle his finger?" He watched BooBoo carefully. "Does he take the match out of his hat:" Collier saw the alarm in the man's eyes and knew that he had accidentally touched on the truth, or part of it. What would a man do with the match? Light it? No, a lot of men lit matches all the time. Chew it? They did that, too. Then he had it. "He takes the match out of his hatband and breaks it in two, and that's the signal."

Powell stared, then shook his head, but he was not denying it; he was indicating his confusion, his discouragement.

"Why don't you sit down here and tell me about it?" Collier invited, moving to the end of the bunk. "You might as well tell us the whole thing since we know most of it already."

"Tell you about what?"

"Let's start with the night Jim Enright was killed. You and Jake were waiting for him along the road, but you're the one who killed him." He held up his hand. "But that's not the important thing, BooBoo. I want to know how you and Jake knew it was Enright who had won a lot of money."

"There was a signal."

"What kind of a signal?"

"A piece of paper. Jake was watching for it while I stayed back from the road with the horses. I used to read, but I can't any more. So Jake waited by the road."

"A man rode along and dropped a piece of paper with Enright's name on it?"

"Somethin' on it," BooBoo said.

Collier slowly got up, his face bleak; he stepped to the door, went out, and let Malloy lock up. The others were waiting on the porch and they looked at him, caught the winter in his eyes.

Then Collier said, "Bill Frame gave the Powell boys the signal to kill Jim Enright."

"My God!" Clayborn said. "Did he tell you that?"

"Without realizing it. He said that he and Jake waited and a man rode by and dropped a piece of paper with Enright's name on it. The only man, beside Enright, who took that road to town that night was Bill Frame."

"I don't think it will stand up in court," Clayborn said. "Frame would hire a good attorney and he'd turn the whole thing into circumstantial evidence. I can inject a reasonable doubt right now. For example, it is possible that another man came along that road. It is possible that someone looked into the window at Spencer's, saw Enright pocket the money, and gave the signal. It is even possible that Spencer gave the signal to someone outside and it was passed on." He shook his head. "I think we're all convinced, but we couldn't convince a jury. Not with BooBoo's testimony."

"Suppose we added Jake's?" Beal said.

Clayborn made a wry face. "Stronger, of course." He looked at Collier. "I'm sorry we have to talk this way but——"

"I want this gang broken up. I'd feel the same way if it was run by my wife." He looked from one to the other. "We know where that room is. In some way, we must trick Frame into going there."

"Well," Beal said, "he wouldn't rise to any bait I threw out."

"Let's not go the rounds," Meers put in. "Gentlemen, with my decayed morals, I'm obviously the man for the job. I could approach Jake with the word that I simply had to talk to the top man and make Jake buy it. After all, I can tell him where his brother is and that will be inducement enough for him. Establish the time for me to move and I'll get Frame into that room. But make sure you're in a position to make an arrest." He smiled wistfully. "After all, Frame may shoot me for this betrayal, and there are a lot of bottles I haven't emptied as yet."

"I hate to keep coming back to BooBoo Powell," Clayborn said, "but, as an attorney, I can appreciate public climate in matters like this. I mean that we need staunch public support and we'd get it by announcing Powell's arrest on the charge of murdering Jim Enright. This will alarm the toughs and perhaps hurry them into making a big mistake. In addition, it will return the police department to favor in the public eyes."

They nodded their agreement. Collier said, "Have Powell brought in and locked up in jail. Clyde, how long will it take you to get a special edition on the street?"

"One page? Four hours."

"I think we know what we're going to do then," Collier said as they went to Clayborn's buggy. He got in and sat there a moment, wishing he were riding back alone; a man needed to be by himself when he felt the way he did—as though everything he had believed was a lie and that he had to start all over again, looking at everyone differently, suspiciously, wondering what there was down inside them that was rotten.

When Meers dropped him off at his gate, Collier walked slowly to the house; June met him on the porch. "I've kept supper warm for you." She opened the door for him, went in ahead of him, and took his plate from the oven. Then she sat down across from him. "You need a shave."

"I need more than that. They're bringing BooBoo Powell to town. The charge is murder. He killed Jim Enright. Bill Frame gave him the signal to do it."

June put her hands to her mouth and her eyes filled with tears. Then she said, "I'm not crying for him, but for you, Adam. You were so different from each other to be friends, but you *were* friends."

He took a bite of food and chewed it listlessly. "Do you know what I was turning over in my mind on the way back?"

"Yes—a way to warn him. To give him a headstart."

He nodded. "Am I so weak that it shows?"

"No, I would say that you're strong enough to be human. What are you going to do, Adam?"

"What can I do? Trap him. See him hung. It's what I'd do to any other man." He went on eating, saying no more about it.

She poured his coffee, then went to answer a knock on the front door. She brought Joe Beal into the kitchen. She offered him coffee; he nodded and sat down.

Collier looked at him and asked, "You surprised to find me here, Joe?"

"No. But stay away from him, Adam. I know you're in the habit of dropping in for a chat." He sighed and added sugar to his coffee. "There are a lot of questions that aren't answered yet. These robberies have netted the toughs a lot of dust. Now you know a man turns that in for coin the first chance he gets, because it's easier to handle, easier to spend, and if a man wasn't a miner and kept a poke full of dust, sooner or later, people would wonder about it. The point is, all that stolen dust had to be changed into coin."

"Frame's saloon would cover that up easy enough," Collier said. "And a lot of the robberies netted coin. No problem there at all." He shook his head. "Frame banks in San Francisco as well as here. He may keep books on the bar business, but the gambling——" He spread his hands. "I don't think there's a chance of catching him in anything, Joe."

"Well, we're going to get him in that cage," Beal said. "I've got a personal reason for hating that thing. As soon as the paper hits the street and we get everybody stirred up, I'm going to quietly close Fat Ella's place."

"He'll hear about that."

"Sure, but he won't think anything of it. I've got one of my policemen all set to get in a brawl there. After he blows his whistle, Ella is as good as out of business. We're going to board up the windows and padlock the doors." He smiled. "Then we're going into the room upstairs and do a little carpentry work so we can see down into the room below, and listen to what goes on there. I've arranged a signal system from the roof; when Frame gets in his cage and Meers is brought in, half the force will surround the house."

"When are you going to do this?"

"Well, I don't know exactly. I'll let you know the minute he's been taken into custody."

"That wasn't what I meant."

"I know what you meant, but maybe I'd better say what I mean. Adam, this is police business and you don't have to be there. In fact, I insist that you stay out of it." He studied the pattern of the tablecloth. "Adam, I've been a man who has been alone most of my life. I never had many close friends. A lot of the people I've worked for, I had very little respect for at all. But I've got a lot of respect for you. I think I had it from the first moment we met because I knew you were a man who would never back down from what was right, no matter how unpopular it was at the time.

"Now, I'm saying this badly," Beal continued, "but what I don't want to see is a time when the friendship you've had for Bill Frame is put to the test. I don't want you there, Adam, not because I'm afraid of anything you'd do, but because I don't want to see you torn apart. That can happen to a man. I've done it to myself. I left the police force in

New York because I was sick of playing crooked politics and being offered handouts. A man wants to do a good job; with some men, that's all they have to offer. Out here, I've been marshal and deputy sheriff and nothing really changed; you played lawman by the local rules, arresting those who were supposed to be arrested, and leaving alone those who ran things. Well, Adam, you've given me a chance to run a real police force, no corruption, no pay-off from anyone. If it goes bust tomorrow, I'll always remember that, for a while, we had real law and order." He got up and smiled. "That arm hurting you much?"

"Not as much as some things."

"That's what I thought," Beal said. "Thanks for the coffee, June."

"You're a nice man," she said. "And they're harder to come by than you think."

Chapter Sixteen

Roan Spencer came to town as soon as he heard about Powell's arrest. It was around ten o'clock, since the paper had come out at eight and it had taken Spencer an hour to get the news and then ride into Bonanza. Roan tied up in front of the hotel, but went across the street to Bill Frame's place and had a drink.

The arrest was causing a lot of excitement because Enright was a well-liked man and the fact that his killer seemed to have gotten away with the murder stuck in a lot of craws. Frame's place was packed with men and noise and he went to the back. He found Frame in his office.

"I thought you'd be in town," Frame said. "That stupid BooBoo—they got a confession from him."

"What about Jake?"

Frame shrugged. "He hasn't been arrested yet. But I suppose BooBoo told them he did it all by himself to cover for Jake. They stick together, those two."

"I don't want to see this come to trial," Spencer said.

"How'll you stop it?"

"Well, if BooBoo isn't alive, they can't try him, can they?"

Frame laughed and fingered his mustache. "Roan, you couldn't get within twenty yards of the jail.

There's policemen all around the place. There's a lot of let's-hang-him-now talk going around town and Beal's making damned sure Powell stays in one piece."

"I was thinking that, maybe at night, four or five policemen could walk right up to the door, jump the ones on duty and get inside. There's bound to be a lot of shooting and you know how it is when the lead starts flying; some innocent man always gets it. BooBoo will never know what hit him."

"Well, I've been having the men lay low since Collier killed those two who attacked him. Roan, that was a damned mistake. And over a game of cards, too."

"No man makes me small," Spencer said flatly. "And I'm not through yet."

"I'll get to work on this," Frame said. "Clayborn is pressing for a quick trial and, with feeling running so high, I'm sure Waller will go along with it. Maybe tonight, late."

"The sooner the better," Spencer said. "If it ends with BooBoo, then we're in the clear; but, if Jake talks, he'll take you down with him, and you'd take me. And I couldn't have that."

"I should be insulted, but I understand your concern. I don't want to hang either." Bill scratched his nose. "Beal closed Fat Ella's place down completely. Boarded it up solid."

"They didn't find the——"

"Naw. Even Collier missed it when he pulled that damned fire inspection some time back."

"I think I'll stay in town tonight," Spencer said. "See that a good job is done."

"How high can I pay?"

"For this one, a thousand dollars a man. But make BooBoo dead."

"You're practically crying at his funeral," Bill Frame said.

Spencer nodded and turned to the door. "Have you seen Adam since the card game?"

"No. If O'Hagen hadn't popped that gun out of his sleeve I'd have——"

"You'd have what? Don't hand me anything, Bill. He had you cold, made a damned fool of you in front of your friend. How am I going to look Adam in the eye again? Hell, I've nursed his friendship for years. You never know when you need a man like him; he'll stand by you when the storm starts to break. How come no one's taken care of O'Hagen anyway?"

"You stay out of town too much," Frame said. "Every one of my men has a pair of cops watching him. Hell, they can't go to the backhouse without Beal getting a report on it. How are you going to move when it's like that?"

"I'd find a way if I was you."

"Hell, take care of O'Hagen yourself. Or can't you do it?"

"I can afford to have someone else do it," Spencer said as he went out.

Frame waited a few minutes, then went out to find Jake Powell; a man said that he was at the jail visiting his brother. Frame sent for him. An hour later Jake Powell showed up, using the side entrance.

"You took your sweet time," Frame told Jake.

"After my brother, you come first."

"Tonight, I want to spring him out of there," Frame said. He outlined his plan. "I want you to stay out of it, Jake. Get four men who haven't been doing anything and have them meet me at the old house at eleven o'clock. You wait at the stable and have two good horses ready. Take a light pack horse along if you're sure it won't slow you down. By the time the smoke dies, I want you and your brother halfway to Arizona. Keep going until you hit Mexico."

"I'll need some money."

"Don't you ever save any? I'll see if I can get you a couple thousand."

"How about two thousand apiece?"

"No," Frame said. "This is a chance for you to get BooBoo out of that jail and clear of the country. Take it or leave it. Besides, I'm paying plenty for those four men. They could get killed, you know."

"All right," Powell said. "What about Fat Ella's place?"

"What about it?"

"Joe Beal closed it up. Ella and her girls are working in some of the houses down the street and Ella swears she's going to take it to the town council."

"Let her. We can still use the place. And if we don't, I'll get someone to set fire to it. The fire department needs the exercise anyway." He waved his hand. "Beat it and be ready to ride. You won't have time to waste."

"It's not easy to see the end of this," Powell said regretfully. "It'll be a long summer before a man gets another thing like this going for him."

"You got your share," Frame said. "Be happy with it."

Jake Powell started to slide the bookcase aside, but stopped when Frame said, "Come back here a minute. Sit down, Jake. I know a man who'd pay two thousand to have someone killed. You could do it tonight about the time the jail was being busted into and still get back to the stable on schedule."

"Who wants it done?"

"What does it matter? How about it?"

"Well, that's a lot of money."

"You'll enjoy it," Frame said. "Adam Collier."

Powell's dark eyes widened and he scratched his unshaven face. "Since this is kind of in a hurry, it'll have to be shoot him and run." He thought about it. "Sure, I'll do it. I never liked him anyway, especially after I had to fix his fence and window." He got up and headed for the side door again. "When do I get paid?"

"Afterward. I'll meet you at the stable with the money."

"All right. But you try anything and——"

"I've always played fair with you," Frame said.

"That's so," Powell admitted and went out.

Frame lit a cigar and poured a drink, then drew a sheet of paper and a pen toward him and wrote for several minutes. Then he reread what he had written, decided to make some corrections, and wrote it again. Satisfied this time, he went out to the bar, collared a man who wasn't doing anything in particular, gave him a dollar, and told him to deliver the note to Adam Collier.

Then Frame went back into his office and laughed.

Adam Collier was at the firehouse on Pass Street when the man from Frame's saloon found him. The messenger had walked across town twice now with the note and, after he handed it to Collier, he stood there as though expecting another dollar. He didn't get it.

Collier unfolded the paper and read:

> My bartenders have big ears; they're trained that way. Jake Powell was in here shooting off his mouth and bragging that he will do someone in tonight. After a few more drinks he let drop that it was on account of his having to paint a fence and fix a window. So take care, huh? Don't stand with your back to a window or door.
>
> BILL

After reading the note again, Collier put it in his pocket, picked up his duck-billed fireman's hat, and walked down Pass to the city jail. Joe Beal was out; the constable on duty said that he was down the street in one of the restaurants; he went out to find him while Collier waited.

When Beal and the constable came back, they went into Beal's office and closed the door.

"Read this," Collier said, handing Beal the note. "What do you make of it?"

"Well, I'd hate to assume it was a lie." He folded the note and held it. "We've got to figure that it would be to Frame's advantage if you were dead, Adam. Another mayor killed right now would throw a scare in a lot of people."

"A thought that crossed my mind—and I'm almost ashamed to say it—is that Jake Powell could tell us a lot. He could point to the head man of the toughs and make it stick. It would be safer for Bill if Jake were dead. You add it up."

Beal rubbed his lean jaw and thought about it. "We've got BooBoo. Jake's been here twice to see him; he keeps telling him he'll get him out someway. It's just talk because I have eight men here at the jail at all times." He squinted his eyes. "Do you suppose that Jake went to Bill and tried to put some weight on him? You know: 'Get my brother out of this or else?' Maybe it was Bill's idea to have Jake try to kill you, then tell you about it so that it worked the other way around."

"He wouldn't do that," Collier said quickly, firmly. "All right, he's lied and robbed, but he wouldn't have me killed. Joe, we soldiered together, fought side by side."

"Yeah, but you're not soldiering now and you haven't for years. You haven't been side by side. Frame's got his life and you've got yours, and they're miles apart. You've gone separate ways, Adam. Face it. You don't know him anymore." He went to the door and said, "Bring me the off-duty sheet." When an officer brought it in, he studied it carefully. "I'll tell you what. I can put six men around your place tonight when it gets dark. If Jake shows up, we can take him, and I want him alive if it's at all possible."

"What do you want me to do?"

"You're not going to do anything," Beal said, "because you're not going to be around."

"Oh, now what the hell——"

Beal smiled. "You've got a broken arm, so I can whip you now, and I will if I have to. I'll even lock you up until this is over if necessary. Now tonight, right after dark, I'll have a man hitch up your buggy and drive your wife and kids out to the ranch; they can stay there until sometime tomorrow—until I tell them they can come home. I'll hide my men around the house, put a sling on one and perch him on the front porch." He jabbed Collier in the chest with his finger. "You can stay right here, out of sight and out of trouble, of your own free will or with an officer detaining you. Take your choice and give me your word now."

"Aw, hell——"

"I'm not fooling."

"I know that." Collier sighed. "All right, I'll stay here. You have my word."

"That's fine," Beal said. "I'll send a man to your house to tell your wife. You stay in here, and I mean in here, not wandering around the building. I'll have your supper sent in with the food for the rest of the prisoners."

"Gee, thanks."

"It's just part of my generous nature," Beal said and they both laughed. He took a key off his ring and handed it to Collier. "This opens the arms locker. Every weapon in there is loaded and ready to fire."

"Do you think I'll need one here?"

Beal got up and walked around the cramped room. "I've been a cop too many years of my life to ignore a crawling feeling in my stomach. It's like one of those hot, sultry days when you sit in the station house and wait for the fire bell to ring. You know?"

"Yes, I know. Is that why you have eight men here at the jail?"

Beal nodded. "I've asked Doc Stover and Clyde Meers to come over after dark."

"How come?"

"Because BooBoo goes on trial in the morning and I wouldn't want him to die from some fatal sickness, like heart trouble, because his heart had a bullet hole in it." Beal got up, stretched, and buttoned his uniform coat. "Sergeant Malloy is in charge of the office and jail while I'm gone. I'll be with my men at your house." He frogged his belt together and put on his cap. "Tonight, the rats are going to come out of their holes. We're going to knock their heads off."

"Don't I even get one little swing?"

Beal shook his head. "You're on the sick list." His smile was quick and deep. He went out, stopping in the outer office to explain everything to Malloy, who went into Beal's office as soon as the chief left the building. He had sergeant's chevrons sewed on his left sleeve.

Collier said, "So the promotions finally got handed out. Three?"

"Aye," Malloy said, making a chair groan under his weight. "It was by pure devotion to duty that I won me hooks. You want to play some cards?"

"How about blackjack?"

"For pennies," Malloy said. "On me present salary, I can't afford more." He produced a deck and shuffled. "Adam, there's a thing I'd like to say to you; I've been wantin' to for a long time."

"Then say it."

"There's been a question in me mind as to whether you'd believe me."

"Try me."

"Because I'm a big mick I've done me share of fightin'. I've had many a proposition, but none like the one Spencer made me that day." He was watching Collier, watching the way his eyes came up quick and alert. "Aye, it was more than a fight Spencer wanted, bucko. He wanted you blind, lad. And made halt and lame. It was to be a fight to cripple you. Or worse."

"Roan is my friend," Collier said softly. "Why——"

He stopped because Malloy was shaking his head slowly. "With a friend like him, a man needs no enemies. It's not clear to me, and perhaps you can put sense to it, but somehow you've wounded the man. He feels he must get even, beat you down." He shoved the cards toward Collier. "You want to cut?"

"No, I don't feel much like playing now."

Chapter Seventeen

When it grew dark, Adam Collier lighted the lamps in Joe Beal's office. He sat alone. He had been sitting alone for two hours, thinking about what Malloy had told him. He knew that Malloy was telling it straight; lying about anything just wasn't one of Malloy's faults.

But he couldn't understand it. Not at all. He had met Roan Spencer a week after he and June and the children had moved to Bonanza. Spencer had been active on the town council then and, right away, several points of contention came up about what kind of a fire department the town was going to have.

Bonanza had been burned to the ground twice in three years and the citizens had had enough of it. They had been convinced that it was cheaper to pay for a fire department than to rebuild the town over and over. Collier, a lieutenant in the Sacramento fire department, had applied for the job, and had been selected. Roan Spencer was full of good ideas, although he had some bad ones too; Collier had argued with him about these and won some decisions and he knew at the time that Spencer hadn't liked it.

Yet they'd become friends and Adam Collier never thought that their differences really mattered.

Spencer liked to cut corners, trying to save a dollar, often risking security in the process.

And Spencer liked to win. He liked to be the best. No one in Bonanza had more money, or a finer home, or better horses and carriages; Roan Spencer was dedicated to being the top man. His wife was always traveling to foreign countries, not because she wanted to go, but because it gave Spencer pleasure to say that she was abroad and that it was costing him a fortune.

Collier and Spencer were not alike. While Collier went about his affairs quietly and efficiently, Spencer always raised a cloud of dust and made a large racket. It wasn't long before Collier understood that Spencer was the dissenting voice in the city government, the eternal fly in the ointment, so, when the opportunity presented itself, Collier put his weight behind Jim Enright and swung the election his way.

Yet he and Spencer had remained friends. At least he had thought so.

Malloy brought in the evening meal on a tray; he got his own dinner and they ate in Beal's office, talked a bit, then Malloy went out and Collier stretched on Beal's cot and tried to get some sleep. His arm ached constantly, a dull throbbing that he was learning to ignore, and he had no trouble falling off.

He woke much later; Malloy was in the room, rattling the lock on the arms locker.

Collier sat up. "What time is it?"

"Nearly midnight." Malloy flung the lock aside and scooped up a half-dozen rifles. "The boys outside report that there are four policemen walking down Gold Street."

"A change of shift?"

"There's no change of shift tonight," Malloy said, cradling the rifles in his big arms. "And I'll tell you one thing, I don't think there's a cop on the force who'd break the rule and walk in any formation except pairs."

He hurried out. And Collier went to the chest and took a sawed-off shotgun and stepped into the outer office.

He heard Malloy speak to the outside guards: "Let 'em come on in." He closed the door and saw Collier. "Would you step back into the cell block with Meers and Stover?" His voice became impatient. "Now hurry, man; they'll be here in a minute."

Collier went back, walking down a barred corridor. Most of the cells contained men detained for various minor offenses and he found Meers and Stover in the last cell, cards scattered on a blanket between them.

"In jail and playing cards," Collier said. "Somehow I knew it would come to this." He glanced in the next cell and saw BooBoo Powell sitting on his bunk, his body in a crouch.

"Why the shotgun?" Stover asked.

"Something's about to——"

He could see down the corridor and the front door was flung open; the four "policemen" burst into the outer office, guns drawn. Instantly, there was a crash of pistol and rifle fire; two of the men sprinted straight down the corridor and one kept shooting back while the leader ran toward BooBoo Powell's cell.

Malloy and his inside men had taken cover; one man was down and another was kneeling, firing his pistol, a hand pressed to a reddening smear on his side. Collier could not tell whether it was one of the regular police force or not.

All this he saw in the space of a second; he made the cell door in one jump, firing the shotgun from the hip. He caught the man just as he was about to shoot into BooBoo's cell. The man spun around and went down, the force of the charge bowling him over backward.

The other man, running full tilt, tripped over the fallen body and rolled just as Collier fired a second time. The charge whanged and scattered harmlessly, then the man came to his hands and knees, smiling, pointing his pistol at Collier.

Then he swung it and shot BooBoo Powell in the forehead a split instant before Malloy cut him down with a rifle shot. The shooting stopped with a suddenness that hurt Collier's ears. He looked around and found Meers and Stover crowded together under the bunk.

Stover crawled out and said, "There's nothing like personal courage in these trying situations, is there?" He saw Powell on the floor, blood oozing from his head. "Good Lord! Open up that cell! Sergeant!"

Malloy came back, one arm hanging limp and bloody. He toed over the dead man, then handed Stover the cell door keys. The doctor hurriedly unlocked the cell and knelt by Powell.

"He's dead."

"So are these two," Malloy said. "I've got another in the outer office, and one who soon will be if you don't patch up the leaks in him." He turned and walked back* weaving slightly; Collier followed him. Malloy spoke to one of his men. "Get that uniform off him. I don't want him lookin' like a cop." He had two men of his own who were wounded; one sat on the floor with a smashed hip and another applied a cloth to a bullet rip on his scalp.

"I've failed in me duty," Malloy said dully. "They killed the prisoner and it was me charge to see that it didn't happen."

"I missed at a time when I couldn't afford to miss," Collier said. "It wasn't your fault, Malloy."

"You're not a cop. It wasn't your duty to defend Powell. It was my responsibility."

Doctor Stover opened his bag and had the wounded men sit on the floor. "You too, Malloy. Come on now. Off with your coat." Meers came from the cell block, composed now and smelling strongly of his private bottle. He helped Stover while Collier had the other policemen take the dead men into one of the empty cells. It was, he thought, like the army; you got into a fire fight, then spent three hours cleaning up, regrouping, pulling the outfit together. This was the weakest moment of man, after a crisis, when he let down; a small boy with a switch could have come in then and whipped them all.

In an hour, the wounded men had been sent, or taken, home. A mop and water was brought in and the floor cleaned up. The dead men were taken in a wagon to Doctor Stover's house; he was the coroner and would have to make out the death certificates.

Collier went to Beal's office, found a bottle and a glass in one of the drawers, and poured himself a stiff drink. His hand shook and the drink helped calm him.

Malloy, refusing to go home, came in, his arm in a sling. He asked, "Are you tryin' to be like me or am I tryin' to be like you?"

"I had mine first."

Malloy tried to smile, but gave up. "I might as well quit," he said. "If a man can't do his duty——"

"Aw, shut up," Collier said. "If you want to feel sorry for someone, feel sorry for BooBoo Powell. The poor, dumb bastard thought they had come to get him out and stood there by the cell door, making a good target of himself." He slapped his hand down on the desk.

"I suppose that's right," Malloy said. "I did feel sorry for the man." He heard a noise outside and jumped to his feet and grabbed up his rifle.

Then Beal and five policemen came in, pushing, dragging Jake Powell who cursed and kicked and writhed. He was shoved into the office and, although he was handcuffed, he tried to kick Beal. Then he turned on Collier who promptly knocked him into a chair with his fist.

Beal saw Malloy's arm and before he could say anything, Malloy made his report, his Voice bleak. Beal's face did not change expression but Jake Powell stopped swearing.

"Dead?" he said. "BooBoo?" He started to get out of the chair and Collier cocked his fist. "No more trouble," Powell said. "No more trouble now. Unlock me. I want a smoke. I mean it, Beal; no more trouble. I've got somethin' to say. Somethin' you want to hear."

Beal produced a key and freed Powell's hands, then gave him a cigar and lit it for him. "Pour him a drink," Beal told Collier. "We caught him trying to climb one of the trees in your front yard. He had a shotgun with solid shot." He took the glass and handed it to Powell. "Now tell us all about it, and make it good."

"How come you knew I was goin' to kill Collier?" Powell asked.

"Bill Frame sent me a note," Collier said. "You want to see it?"

"No, I believe it. All right, I ain't dead. I'm supposed to be, but I ain't. Frame was goin' to give me two thousand dollars to kill you, Collier. But now I see what he had in mind. I was to do the job and then get killed myself. Nice, huh? Nobody to talk." He held up the glass. "Can I have another?"

Beal nodded and Collier poured it, then put the bottle on the desk and waited.

Jake Powell sat hunched in the chair, rubbing his wrists. "I guess I'm going to hang, huh? Well, it's somethin' I always expected, kind of. I wouldn't have let BooBoo hang alone anyway." He looked at Beal. "Sure, he swung the lead pipe and broke Enright's head, but he wasn't all there, you understand, and he just didn't know how hard to hit a man. We never intended to kill Enright or anyone else. Hittin' 'em on the head's all right, but people get all riled up when there's a killin'."

"That does seem to be a fact," Beal said dryly. "What did you do with the money you took off Enright?"

"Gave it to Frame. He got all the money from the robberies and I did the payin' off. He never showed himself to anyone but me."

"How come *you*?" Collier asked. "Exposure was something he didn't want, so why did he trust you?"

"On account of BooBoo," Jake Powell said. "I've been takin' care of him since the accident. Only thing was, I just couldn't work at a regular job. People were always havin' fun with him. You know, gettin' him to do crazy things because he didn't know better and always gettin' him in trouble. We'd been kicked out of a few towns because they'd get him to grab some woman on the street and things like that. I just couldn't work steady at a job and take care of him too." He looked at Beal. "Another drink?"

"You can have the bottle after you're through. How did you meet Bill Frame?"

"About three years ago, I saw a man win heavy at his place. So I jumped him in the alley and, before I knew it, one of his roughnecks piled on me. He heard the commotion and came out, then took me inside and talked to me. I thought he was goin' to have me done in, but he told me about an organization he was trying to set up, a dozen picked men to work as a team, on salary; that's the way he put it. I was to handle the pickin' of the men, make the payments to 'em, and set up the things we had to do. As long as I did all right, he'd see that me and BooBoo were taken care of. He kept his word, until now."

Beal opened the door and spoke to one of the officers. "Go get Clayborn."

"He's in bed asleep, Chief."

"Damn it! I don't care if he's havin' good luck with his wife, get him here." He closed the door and turned to Jake Powell. "You'll have to swear to this in court."

"I'll swear to it."

"How come you tried to climb the tree? That was pretty stupid."

Powell grinned. "I seen Collier—or a man I thought was Collier—sittin' on the porch. I figured that if he saw me tryin' to climb the tree he'd come out to see what the hell I was doin'. If I'd sneaked around he'd figured he was in danger, but a man who climbs a tree must be drunk or somethin'. When he got close, I was goin' to let him, have both barrels."

Collier said, "Jake, you're a hell of a nice guy."

"Well, I don't know," Powell said, "I've done some mean things in my time. That's a fact."

"It's hard to believe," Collier said, his manner disgusted. "Give him his bottle and let him drink himself into a stupor."

"Not quite yet," Beal said. "Who set up the attack on the jail?"

"I did." He wiped a hand across his unshaven chin. "They were goin' to get BooBoo out. We had horses waitin' at the stable and we were goin' to clear out of the country. I didn't know they were to kill him."

Beal asked, "Jake, you got the little end of the stick all around, didn't you?" He reached for pencil and paper. "I want the names of every tough who's ever worked for you and Frame. Give me his name and tell me where we can find him."

"There's only about seven left." He sighed and told Beal their names and the places they could be found.

"Now, where do you keep the police uniforms?"

"Well, they're all gone now so——"

"Answer me!"

Powell frowned and shifted in his chair. "We used the back shed behind Jim Enright's old house. Since his wife moved away, the place has been vacant, and Frame thought it would be a good place."

Clayborn arrived slightly out of breath. As soon as he entered the room, Joe Beal said, "Get Judge Waller out of bed. I want a warrant sworn out for Bill

Frame. Make up what charges you think will stick. Tell him—never mind. Malloy, go with him, and tell the judge what's happened here tonight. If he wants to go ahead with the trial, we can try Jake instead of BooBoo."

Beal took the bottle off the desk and tossed it into Powell's lap, then flung open the door and called in the jailer. "Lock this man up and throw away the key."

Chapter Eighteen

The gunfight at the jail attracted so much attention that the arrest of Jake Powell went completely unnoticed; within fifteen minutes of the smoke clearing, everyone in town believed that three policemen had been killed and four of them wounded, one so badly that he was dying, and no one was aware that the dead and dying were part of the gang of toughs.

Clyde Meers returned to his newspaper office and locked the door, and, without once taking a drink, worked all night, driving his printer's devil to a frenzy of activity.

At eight o'clock, his newspaper was given to a half-dozen delivery boys. Meers sat down at his desk and uncorked his bottle, satisfied that he would never put out an edition of the paper better than this one.

There was a two-column account of the toughs' raid on the jail and the killing of BooBoo Powell. Beside it, a column-and-a-half account of Jake Powell's attempted assassination of his honor, the mayor, and his subsequent arrest by officers who were waiting in the vicinity of Collier's house.

Filling out the page, was a large box edged in black, an editorial, a stern warning to the toughs. They were through in Bonanza. A rope awaited those who might be foolish enough to linger on in this unhealthy climate.

Roan Spencer, up early, bought a paper, read it completely, abandoned his half-eaten meal and left the hotel. He started to cut across the street to the Jackpot, then stopped on the porch when he saw the two policemen standing on either side of the door. After a brief hesitation, Spencer walked down the street and, at the corner, cut over. As he cleared the traffic and reached the walk, he saw the policeman standing at the end of the alley. Without going any further, Spencer knew that there was another at the other end, sealing off the block.

He turned and walked on down toward the Jackpot and mounted the porch. Judging from the noise inside, business was brisk. Spencer went in, paused at the bar for a drink and a look around, then went into the back to Frame's office.

He went in without knocking. Frame quickly pointed a gun at him, then put it away. He wore no coat and there was a sheen of sweat on his forehead.

Spencer said, "You're a damned fool, Bill. There are cops all around this place. Jake talked his head off." He pulled up a chair and sat down. "I don't blame him. After reading the newspaper, I can see what you tried to pull. He'll take you along with him now just to get even." Then he smiled and reached into his pocket for his cigar case. "But I came here to help you, Bill. Here, have a cigar." He extended the case.

Frame put down his pistol and reached for a cigar. Before he could think, Spencer scooped up the gun and pointed it at Frame's forehead. Then he got up, slowly walked around the desk, the muzzle never wavering. Frame sat there, cigar laxly held, his mouth open.

"A man like you, an officer and a gentleman, has to do the honorable thing," Spencer said as he hit Frame with the barrel of the gun.

The blow was not delivered with enough force to knock Frame out, but it stunned him, and he slumped in the chair, groggy, and unable to resist.

Quickly, Spencer put the pistol in Frame's hand, pressed the muzzle against his temple, and using his hand over Frame's, pressed the trigger. The .44 boomed in the closed room and Frame's head jumped. There was the strong odor of burned hair and black powder. Then Spencer was out of the office, running wildly through the saloon, yelling that Frame had committed suicide.

He was a thoroughly shocked and unnerved man. When Beal and Adam Collier arrived, Spencer had still not completely recovered; he sat slumped in a chair, whiskey before him, a blank, incredulous look in his eyes.

Beal had him taken down the street to his office. Policemen were brought in to restore order and to close the place. Stover was busy, so Doctor Ainsley was sent for and, as soon as Beal could detach himself, he walked back to his office with Adam Collier.

Spencer was more composed now, but his hands still shook slightly when he wiped them across his face. Beal seemed very relaxed and in no particular hurry; he sat down and lit a cigar.

"You were with Frame when he killed himself?"

Spencer nodded. "We were talking. The gun was

on his desk. He was very tense, disturbed. Then he picked up the gun and shot himself in the temple."

Collier opened his mouth to say something, but Beal shook his head slightly, so Collier remained silent. Beal watched Spencer.

"What were you doing in there, Mr. Spencer?" Beal asked.

"Doing? Why, Bill and I were friends. I'd just read the paper at breakfast and went over to see what he thought of it. We'd always talked about the day when the toughs would be gone and Bonanza would be a decent place to live."

"You left the table in a hurry," Beal pointed out. "You didn't finish your breakfast and you forgot to pay for it."

"Did I? Well, they'll put it on my bill." He looked at Adam Collier. "I'm sorry, Adam. This must be a special shock to you; I know you and Bill had been friends for a long time."

"What did Frame say before he shot himself?" Beal asked.

"He didn't make much sense," Spencer admitted. "He said he just couldn't face it. Then he picked up the gun and pulled the trigger."

Beal took a cigar from his pocket. "Roan, this was picked up off the floor. One of yours, isn't it?"

Spencer nodded. "I offered it to him. He took it." He put his face in his hands. "It was awful, a man doing away with himself that way."

"Then Frame never admitted being the leader of the toughs?"

"No. I didn't know what he was talking about. The truth didn't dawn on me until I sat down here."

He looked from one to the other. "Who'd have guessed it? I mean, here's a man with a good business, a bright, nice fella. You'd just never think——" Spencer shook his head and stared at the floor.

Joe Beal sat there and puffed his cigar; he let two minutes pass, three.

Finally, Spencer looked at him and asked, "What did you bring me here for?"

"It's a nice quiet place to talk," Beal said. "Does it make you nervous, being in a jail?"

"Well, I've never been in jail." He looked at Adam Collier. "What do you keep looking at me for?"

"Is there anything wrong with that?"

"You both keep looking at me," Spencer said. "I've been through a hell of an experience, I can tell you. It really shakes a man."

Spencer stopped talking when Sean O'Hagen came in. Sean drew Beal to one side and talked in whispers, rolling his eyes in Spencer's direction. Then he went out and Beal sat on the corner of his desk and studied Spencer.

"Roan, right after we arrested BooBoo, we knew that Frame was the man behind the toughs. We knew that he had pointed his finger at Jim Enright for the kill."

"BooBoo seen him, huh?"

Beal shook his head. "BooBoo said that someone coming from your place dropped a note for Jake, and the only other man on that road besides Enright was Frame. That's how we knew."

"Then why didn't you arrest him?" Spencer asked. "What kind of a policeman are you?" He looked from one to the other. "What'd the gambler want?"

"He was just reporting to me," Beal said. "Like I

said, we've been watching Frame pretty close since we found out he was boss." He paused and puffed on his cigar. "You want to tell us how Bill got that cut on his head, Roan?"

Spencer swallowed. "Maybe he hit it when he fell."

"He didn't fall," Beal commented. "He just slumped over in his chair. That's the way you left him and that's the way he was when we found him. Yet he had this cut on his head like someone had hit him. That's what I'm asking about, Roan."

"Why, I don't know nothing about it. I don't know anything at all."

"All right," Beal said casually. "What did you mean when you told Frame that you could see what he tried to pull and that Jake would take him along just to get even?" He raised his eyes and they locked with Spencer's. "O'Hagen's been hiding in the room above Frame's office; he disconnected the stove pipe so he could hear everything that went on. Want to tell me about it, Roan? You knew Bill was heading the toughs. We know it, so why deny it?"

"Are you arresting me?"

"No, because we've already talked with Clayborn and Judge Waller and we couldn't get a conviction." He got up off his desk and opened the door. "You're free to go, Roan, but remember something: there'll always be a lot of eyes on you, watching what you do, where you go. You'll make a mistake, Roan; your kind always does. I'd like to hang you for Bill Frame's murder, but I just haven't got enough evidence. Maybe I never will have it, but I'm not going to be too disappointed about it; I've learned that you can't win 'em all." He motioned toward the door. "Go on, get out of here."

Spencer looked at Adam Collier. "You don't believe this, do you?"

"Yes. Frame worked for you or you worked for him; I'm not sure which way it was, Roan, but you're a died-in-the-wool crook. What would you do, Roan, if a rumor got started that you'd murdered Frame to cover up your own part in the organization?" Collier smiled thinly. "You know how talk gets started, Roan, and it's hell to stop." He reached out and thumped Spencer on the chest. "You hate like hell to be beaten at anything, but I'll tell you something: you'll never beat me. You'll never find a man to do it with his fists and you have no real guts, so I don't think you'll do it with a gun. All you can do is to look at me and know that I can see the truth about you—a big tub of guts, all mouth and wind, with nothing but greed to keep you going." Collier reached out and roughly shoved Spencer toward the door. "Go on, get out of here like you've been told! You stink up a place."

Spencer reeled to the door, caught his balance, then whirled and pointed his finger at Collier. "Bang," he said. "That's the way you're going to get it. Bang! Bang!"

Then he plunged out, bumping a policeman by the door.

Collier stood by the window, watching him hurry along. Beal stood beside him and said, "He'll find someone, Adam, some stupid gunman."

"Well, we know it so we can be watching. This will eat on him; I know the man now. Finally, he'll make his mistake. We've just got to be waiting for it." He turned away from the window. "Did you have my wife and kids brought back to town yet?"

"They're on their way now," Beal said. He drew on the stub of his cigar then butted it out. "A man feels a little let down. You know? You think it'll end with a roar, and instead you get a whimper. The public will be a little disappointed they didn't get at least one hanging out of this."

Collier shrugged. "None of us get what we really want, do we?"

"Guess not." Beal rubbed his cheek. "It'll be a quiet town. I suppose now the town council will want to cut back the police force. If they do, it'll be wide open again in two months." He turned again to the window. "You look out there at all those people on the street and you wonder what's going on in their heads—which one is thinking of taking over where Bill Frame left off. He's out there, walking around, with it all locked in his head. He's out there, and a man never really stops hunting, does he?"

"No," Collier said. "And I'll look into faces now, faces of men I think I know, and I'll wonder what's behind their eyes. I've learned to do that, and I don't like it. But I know I will do it. Know I have to." He sighed and buttoned his coat. "Why don't you come over for supper tonight; June would love to have you."

"Some other time," Beal said. "Go back to living for awhile, Adam. Go fishing with your kids or hunting jack rabbits. Men like you and I have to do things like that so we can get our faith in people back again. We see a lot of dirt and, if we don't watch it, we get to thinking everyone's corrupt."

"You think that'll work?"

"I think it's worth a try," Beal said honestly.

Wade Everett, a pseudonym for Will Cook, is the author of numerous outstanding Western novels as well as historical frontier fiction. He was born in Richmond, Indiana, but was raised by an aunt and uncle in Cambridge, Illinois. He joined the U.S. cavalry at the age of sixteen but was disillusioned because horses were being eliminated through mechanization. He transferred to the U.S. Army Air Force in which he served in the South Pacific during the Second World War. Cook turned to writing in 1951 and contributed a number of outstanding short stories to *Dime Western* and other pulp magazines as well as fiction for major smooth-paper magazines such as *The Saturday Evening Post*. It was in the *Post* that his best-known novel, *Comanche Captives*, was serialized. It was later filmed as *Two Rode Together* (Columbia, 1961) directed by John Ford and starring James Stewart and Richard Widmark. It has now been restored, as was the author's intention, with *The Peacemakers* set in 1870 as the first part and *Comanche Captives* set in 1874 as the second part of a major historical novel titled *Two Rode Together*. Sometimes in his short stories Cook would introduce characters that would later be featured in novels, such as Charlie Boomhauer who first appeared in *Lawmen Die Sudden* in *Big-Book Western* in 1953 and is later to be found in *Badman's Holiday* (1958) and *The Wind River Kid* (1958). Along with his steady productivity, Cook maintained an enviable quality. His novels range widely in time and place, from the Illinois frontier of 1811 to southwest Texas in 1905, but each is peopled with credible and interesting characters whose interactions form the backbone of the narrative. Most of his novels deal with more or less traditional Western themes—range wars, reformed outlaws, cattle rustling, Indian fighting—but there are also romantic novels such as *Sabrina Kane* (1956) and exercises in historical realism such as *Elizabeth, by Name* (1958). Indeed, his fiction is known for its strong heroines. Another common feature is Cook's compassion for his characters who must be able to survive in a wild and violent land. His protagonists make mistakes, hurt people they care for, and sometimes succumb to ignoble impulses, but this all provides an added dimension to the artistry of his work.